Rolf's arms clamped down like a blacksmith's vise, and Raider could feel white-hot pain shoot through his already damaged ribs, as though a smith's super-heated mandrel had been shoved inside his body.

A few more seconds of this, Raider knew, and Rolf would kill him for sure.

Raider had no leverage and no time. He had to do something *now.*

He threw himself backward, taking Rolf with him.

Raider felt the sharp drop of the riverbed under his boots, and he shoved back with all the strength he had.

Icy, foaming water closed over them both and, still locked in Rolf's crushing grip, Raider and his enemy were spun toward the roaring torrent of the white-water rapids.

# THE COLORADO STING

BERKLEY BOOKS, NEW YORK

THE COLORADO STING

A Berkley Book/published by arrangement with
the author

PRINTING HISTORY
Berkley edition/July 1985

ISBN: 0-425-07974-0

A BERKLEY BOOK ® TM 757,375
Berkley Books are published by The Berkley Publishing Group,
200 Madison Avenue, New York, N.Y. 10016.
The name "BERKLEY" and the stylized "B" with design are trademarks
belonging to Berkley Publishing Corporation.

# THE COLORADO STING

# CHAPTER ONE

The man known as Jason Jones grinned and drew in another pile of winnings from the green-felt-covered table.

"You're too damn much for me, mister," one of the other players said with disgust. The man gathered what money he had left on the table, pocketed it, and left the table.

Jones shrugged and reached for the cards. He began to shuffle them, leaving his winnings uncounted and unsorted in a glittering heap on the table before him. There was a good-sized pile of metal there, and most of it gleamed yellow in the lamplight from the bright fixtures overhead. There were only three men left in the game now, and two of them had been reduced to small, cautious betting by the success Jones had had during the evening's play. If Jones minded, though, he didn't show it.

"May I join you?" a fourth man asked, approaching the

table. The newcomer was tall and slender and elegantly dressed. His hair, carefully brushed, showed silver in the light of the ceiling lights, and he brought with him a faint scent of bay rum or some other expensive toilet water.

One of the men grunted and pointed towards Jones. "If you c'n break his spell, mister, you're damn sure welcome."

"I know. I've been watching," the newcomer said. He smiled. "Challenge intrigues me. Would you mind, sir?"

"Me?" Jones asked. "Not at all. The idea's to have some fun, right? An' anyway, your money's as good here as anybody's." His voice did not match his appearance, which was quite as elegant as that of the newcomer to the table.

The man called Jones introduced himself, and the new player looked him over carefully, as if assessing more than an opponent for an evening with the cards.

What he saw was a tall man, probably several inches above six feet. Jones was trimly built but well muscled beneath an expensively cut suit coat. He had dark eyes surrounded by sun-wrinkled skin that had been tanned by wind and weather. He wore a full beard, equally dark, and his hair was as black as a raven's wing. The beard was short and handsomely groomed, the portion of it between lip and nose somewhat fuller, as if until recently he had worn not a beard but a mustache lately trimmed to match the newer growth of full beard.

He wore a waistcoat and tie in addition to the finely cut and unsoiled suit. His stickpin was mounted with a glittering bauble that was suspiciously large to be a real diamond. He wore an equally gaudy ring on the little finger of his left hand.

Not everything Jones wore seemed to be there for the sake of appearance, though. The use-polished grips of a .44-caliber Remington revolver showed at his waist where his suit coat fell away from the chair. And there was an air of rugged competence about him that belied the soft and gentlemanly impression his clothing tried to present.

The newcomer smiled again and introduced himself. "Charles LeFarge," he said. He pronounced it in the French fashion, with a sibilant "sh" sound at the beginning of his first name.

"Folks call you Charlie, do they?" Jones asked.

LeFarge's smile tightened slightly. "Most refer to me as Mr. LeFarge."

Jones chuckled and began to deal the cards. "All right, Mr. LeFarge. You c'n call me Mr. Jones."

"As you wish."

"The game, Mr. LeFarge, is draw poker. Nothin' wild, an' you can open on nerve or anything better you got to back it up. The ante is five dollars. Which I notice you seem to be light on."

LeFarge colored slightly. He reached into his coat pocket for a small, tooled leather purse and spilled a quantity of gold double eagles onto the table in front of him. The other men had already anted with five-dollar half eagles. LeFarge pushed a twenty-dollar piece into the middle of the table and pulled back the other three coins to make change for himself. Jones nodded. Only then did any of the others feel free to pick up their cards and see what fate—and Mr. Jones—had dealt them.

The wiry man to Jones's left, who had the pasty complexion of an underground miner who rarely sees daylight, snorted in disgust and threw his hand in immediately. His friend, seated across the table from Jones, paid another five dollars for two cards before he tossed in a pair of deuces. Jones held his pat hand. So did LeFarge.

"Well, Mr. LeFarge?"

"Twenty dollars, Mr. Jones?"

Jones grinned. He tossed a double eagle into the pot. Then another.

LeFarge kicked in his twenty and laid down two pair, eights over treys. Jones laughed loudly, loud enough for the sound to be heard throughout the large and busy gaming room. He laid down three tens and raked the pot in.

"Your luck is remarkable, Mr. Jones," LeFarge said.

"Ain't it just," Jones agreed. "Specially since it seems to happen no matter who's dealin'." He laughed again and motioned toward one of the fancy girls who was circulating through the room. "You there, missy. What's your name, honey?"

She came to their table and ran her fingertips along the back of Jones's neck. "Marcia," she said. "What's your name, cutey?"

He told her but added, "We'll talk about that sorta thing later, honey. Right now I'd like you to set my friends here up to somethin' to drink. Whatever they want. Can you do that for me, honey?"

"Sure thing, Jason. Whatever you want." She smiled, and Jones sent her on her way toward the bar at the other end of the long room.

"A toothsome morsel," LeFarge observed as the girl wiggled her way through the crowd.

"Huh?"

"Nice," LeFarge explained.

Jones grinned. "Yeah. Or so it seems." He winked. "Tell you more later, eh?"

"Yes. Quite." LeFarge reached inside his coat and brought out a long cigar with a pale and obviously expensive wrapping leaf. "Care for one?"

The man at Jones's left accepted one, and so did his companion. Jones only made a face and shook his head.

LeFarge shrugged. "To each his own pleasures, what?"

"Yeah, whatever you say." The girl came back with a bottle and four glasses. Jones gave her a five-dollar gold piece and told her to keep the change. He tossed another half eagle into the middle of the table and said, "Hey, are we playin' or not here?"

"We're playing," one of the other men said. They all anted, and the play went on.

The two miners played cautiously and therefore, predictably, lost. Their losses were small but steady, their wins infrequent and also small. The game seemed mostly to be played between Jones and LeFarge, with Jones having a slight edge in the number of pots taken but LeFarge usually able to win the larger pots.

After one particularly large pot—large, at least, for this game—it was LeFarge's turn to call the girl Marcia to their table.

"We could use a snack, Miss Marcia of the lovely green eyes," he said. "Something beyond the ordinary run of the free lunch fare. Something, um, with some zest to it. An hors d'oeuvre of quality, eh? Would you have caviar, perhaps?"

She laughed. "In Leadville? Mister, you got to be kidding."

LeFarge smiled and shrugged. "Then do your best, lass. See what you might find. A tidbit with presence, as it were."

The girl left and the play resumed. LeFarge dealt Jones a winning hand, and one of the miners dropped out of the game. "Too much for me," the man said. His companion stayed for one hand more, then picked up the little cash he had left in front of him and went off in the direction his partner had just taken.

"Time to become serious, Mr. Jones?" LeFarge asked.

Jones grinned at him. "Whatever pleases you, Sharles."

LeFarge nodded and anted with a twenty-dollar double eagle. No one else in the busy room seemed interested in joining them at that level.

Marcia returned with a doubtful expression and a clean but somewhat tarnished silver tray. The tray held an assortment of small crackers and a dish of dark, smoked oysters swimming in a greasy, smelly substance. LeFarge beamed when he saw them.

"Perfect," the silver-haired man said.

"You're sure you wanta eat this stuff, mister?" the girl asked, her skepticism in her voice now as well as on her face.

"Quite as good as caviar," LeFarge assured her.

"That's what the cook tol' me, but..." She shrugged, accepted payment from LeFarge, and went away.

LeFarge offered the tray to Jones, but the big, darkly handsome gambler shook his head.

"Not to your taste, sir?"

"Delicate stomach," Jones explained. He covered his mouth with a fist and belched into it just from thinking about the heavy oil that coated the oysters. LeFarge looked oddly satisfied by the response. With obvious pleasure he speared one of the small oysters with a tiny silver fork provided on the tray, balanced it on a scrap of cracker, and popped the delicacy into his mouth.

"Um. Excellent," he said.

Jones belched again and began shuffling the cards.

Jones pushed his chair back from the table and pulled a turnip-shaped watch from his vest pocket. He looked at the watch, tucked it back into the pocket, and began gathering his winnings into a neat pile.

"Quitting so early?" LeFarge asked.

"Been a long day," Jones told him. He added a wink and said, "And it ain't over yet."

"Perhaps tomorrow night then, sir?"

"Could be," Jones said. He turned and motioned for Marcia. When she reached the table he reached down and separated one gleaming double eagle from the pile in front of him, then scooped the rest of the money into his coat pocket. "Got time for a sashay upstairs, pretty lady?" The amount of money was an extravagant overpayment for her services. One tenth of it would have been enough to claim her time for a quickie. Half would have bought her for the night or what was left of it. She giggled when she accepted the twenty-dollar gold piece and clutched the coin tight in her fist. Jones gave LeFarge another wink and let the girl lead him up the banistered stairway toward the private rooms above. He walked close behind her and once in full view of the room full of men reached out to squeeze the girl's ample rump with a large hand. She squealed and laughed as she went up on tiptoes and hurried on ahead of her obviously amorous customer.

They reached the top of the stairs, and Marcia led the way to the back of the long, narrow, two-story structure. She opened the door and let Jones inside, then closed and bolted the door behind them.

Immediately she slipped the top of her short, scarlet dress off her shoulders and let the bodice fall to her waist, exposing large but wrinkled and blue-veined breasts that had already begun to sag although she looked to be little more than twenty.

"Anything you want, honey," she was saying with a professional smile of welcome.

But Mr. Jones was no longer the gay, glad-handing gambler he had appeared downstairs. In fact, Mr. Jones was paying no attention whatsoever to his recent purchase.

With his right hand riding close to the butt of the Remington, he double-checked the bolt across the door and reached up to make sure the transom above was closed and locked.

Then, still ignoring Marcia, he turned and crossed the small room in three long strides to reach the shuttered window that overlooked a littered alley behind the building.

"Jones" unlocked the shutters and pushed them open. He pushed up the window. One or both of the sash weights that were suppose to balance the weight of the window and frame had come loose. Jones had to find something to prop the window open. He made do with a knitting needle he found on the small table in front of the window, then moved the table aside so it wouldn't block the window.

Marcia looked confused. "What are you . . ." Then comprehension crossed her face. "You're *him!*"

"Uh huh," the man called Jones said absently. He looked at her for the first time since they had entered the room. "Pull your dress up, girly. An' then you might want to go bounce on those bedsprings or something." He chuckled. "In case somebody's listening."

"Geez, mister, I didn't have no idea you was the one I'd been told about." She opened her hand and looked down at the coin that glistened in her palm. She sighed.

Raider laughed. "Keep it, honey. We got a big budget to play with for a change here, an' it wouldn't do none for you not to have the money folks've seen me pay you."

The girl looked considerably happier after that. "You want me t' moan an' groan some too, mister?"

"Whatever," Raider said. "Mostly we'll want you to keep your ears an' your mouth shut whenever I come up here to have a romp with my favorite tootsie." He winked at her.

Marcia looked again at the coin in her palm, then apparently decided to press her luck while it was running so strong. "You're really gonna do right by my Jackie, mister?"

Raider made a face. "Honey, far as I'm concerned, your darlin' Jackie can sit in that jail till he grows moss on his balls. That don't make no nevermind to me at all. But the people in charge o' this say they won't prosecute him if you do your part the way you promised an' give me a way to meet my partner in private."

The conversation was interrupted by a faint scratching noise from outside the open window.

A moment later a fat, elderly man—a bum, really, to judge by his clothing—scrambled with remarkable agility down from the roof to the windowsill. The fat man moved with exceptional ease and grace for his ungainly appearance.

Raider grinned and held the window higher while Doc Weatherbee crawled through and joined him in the privacy of the whore's small room.

# CHAPTER TWO

The two men shook hands, and Doc immediately began peeling away some of the layers of thick cotton padding that helped transform him from a merely slightly plump man into a fat, disreputable drunk, as he now was appearing for the world's benefit.

Raider chuckled and wrinkled his nose. "Kinda ripe, ain't you?"

Doc made a sour face, almost sour enough to match the smell that clung to his ragged clothes. "I told that imbecile that he was placing us in the wrong roles here. I am certainly the logical choice to portray a gentleman." He gave Raider a hard look. "And you, certainly, would have been at home as a beggar on the streets." He sniffed haughtily, then seemed to regret it as the odors of his own person assaulted him. "God, but it's hot in this miserable outfit. Thank heaven for the cool nights at this elevation."

9

Raider adopted an innocent expression. "Orders, Mr. Weatherbee. We are all required to follow them with good cheer and diligence." He laughed.

"Good cheer and diligence, my ass," Doc said. "If I didn't know better I might think some of your act is rubbing off on you."

"Shee-it," Raider said.

"That sounds more like you." Doc let the bottommost layers of cotton flop open and used his hat—which looked like it had recently been used to mop up the floor of a stable—to fan some fresh air toward his sweating frame.

Behind them on the bed, unnoticed and virtually forgotten for the moment, Marcia sat staring at the odd pair. Her interest was so complete that she had forgotten to moan and groan for the time being.

"This whole thing is your fault," Doc complained. "If you were any kind of decent operative, the agency could trust you to maintain communications. As usual, though, I have to be the one to cover for you."

"Why, you sorry, ungrateful son of a bitch," Raider returned. "Here I'm the one puttin' it on the line, as usual, while you sit back an' take life easy. As usual."

Doc ignored the outburst, but his eyes did seem to twinkle slightly in appreciation of the reaction he had gotten. "I don't suppose you were thoughtful enough to provide a poor old man with something to ease his thirst," he said. "No," he answered his own question, "you wouldn't have done that." He turned to the girl, not giving Raider time to say anything in response, and said, "You would be Marcia, of course."

She nodded. She seemed not to know quite how to take this unlikely, mismatched pair of Pinkerton men who had invaded her quarters.

"You may be interested to know," Doc said, "that I saw your, uh, fiancé as recently as yesterday morning. He appears to be well and in good spirits, considering."

"He doesn't know—"

Doc shook his head. "He has no idea that you are cooperating with us. Nor should he, I remind you. Which is why I bring the subject up now, young lady. Your letter to him has been intercepted."

"But I didn't—"

Doc held up a hand to cut her off. "Not specifically, no, but there were certain hints about his freedom. Not even that much, if you please. He must know nothing about this. No one can, or Raider's life will be in jeopardy here."

Marcia looked confused. "Who the hell is Raider?"

Doc hooked a thumb toward the gentleman in question, better known in Leadville now as Jason Jones.

"Oh."

Raider bowed toward the girl after the sort-of introduction.

Weatherbee laughed. "If a man has no manners," he said, "I suppose it is an acceptable substitute for him to ape them."

"Up your ass, Weatherbee."

Doc grinned. "Perhaps the substitution is not entirely acceptable, then."

Raider removed his coat and dropped it onto the foot of the bed beside the girl. He unfastened the buttons of his vest and pulled the knot of his tie away from his Adam's apple. With a sigh of relief he helped himself to the only available seat in the room, on the bed next to the girl. "Are you going to get down to business or not?"

Doc's expression became more serious. He glanced once at the girl.

"Unavoidable," Raider said.

"I suppose so." Doc dropped his hat onto the floor—it certainly couldn't become any more soiled or foul than it already was—and sat as well. Both men ignored Marcia.

"Have you made contact?" Doc asked.

Raider grinned at him. "Easy as gettin' a possum to eat shit," he said.

"Did he recognize you?"

Raider shrugged. "Hard to say. If he did he never gave any sign of it."

Doc grunted.

"What about you?" Raider asked.

Doc shrugged. "As expected. I can't use the telegraph here, of course. Not and maintain my cover as your watchdog. But I can hop the rails down to Buena Vista to get messages off or go over the pass to Mosquito Gulch if need be."

"The drop in Buena Vista's been established?"

Doc nodded. "Under the name Olaf Hansen, if you need to use it. The telegraph operator has no idea what this Mr. Hansen is supposed to look like. And of course any emergency messages will be coded."

"Won't do no good if they are," Raider said pessimistically. "Smart as this son of a bitch seems to be, he'd have it figgered anyhow."

"Not this time," Doc said. "This time we take him down for a long count."

"I don't know," Raider said. "Time an' time again the bastard's come away clean."

"But not this time."

Raider chuckled. "The damn railroads'd be mad as hell if he slips outta this one, what with the bundle they've put on it. Come to think of it, old tightwad Pinkerton wouldn't be none too happy even if it ain't his money going down the shithouse hole."

"But this time he falls," Doc said.

"They've thought that before."

"Perhaps, but this time I am on the job."

"You! You sorry ol' cocksucker. I have to do all the hard work, an' you're already looking to take the credit for it."

Doc smiled.

"Seriously, though," Raider said, "I don't know as this thing is gonna work. Too damn complicated."

"It can work, damn it," Doc insisted. "The word is already being put out. Very quietly, of course, but where we know it will do some good. Rumors. A very unofficial pickup and hold request given to certain officers of the law. That sort of thing. If the man is half as good as he is reputed to be, he could not possibly fail to know about the rumors."

"Too damn complicated," Raider said again.

"The man is simply too wary of anything simple," Doc said, adding, "anything you might devise, for instance." The jibe missed its mark, going over Raider's head in his preoccupation with the complexity of their current mission for the Pinkerton National Detective Agency.

"Too damn complicated," Raider repeated.

"Just do your job, Rade," Doc said. "Let the men who are paying the bills worry about the complexities. All right?"

Raider shrugged, but he still looked skeptical.

Doc turned to the girl, who had been listening intently to the conversation although she probably didn't understand a quarter of it. "You haven't heard anything, of course."

"No, sir," she said. Belatedly she remembered what she was supposed to be doing. She began to bounce on the bed and moan loudly.

Doc shook his head. Raider's idea of stealth and deception, he supposed. Although anyone interested enough to already be listening outside the door would long since have had an earful when two male voices were heard within the room.

He bent and retrieved his hat, made a face at it, and yanked it down over his ears. He stood and began to refasten the layers of padding and the smelly clothing that burdened him on this assignment. He gave Raider's handsomely cut suit an envious glance while he did so.

And then that damned Raider had the effrontery to make a similarly sour face when he tugged the knot of his tie back where it belonged.

"When do you want to meet again?" Doc asked.

"Two nights from now. Same time?"

Doc nodded. He gave his costume a final going-over to make sure everything was as it should be—the look was hardly one of approval—and crossed to the window. "See you then," he said.

Raider held the window for him while Doc slipped outside into the chill night air and scrambled lightly up onto the flat roof of the tall, false-fronted building.

# CHAPTER THREE

Charles LeFarge hurried out of the saloon and across the street to the Sloan House, one of Leadville's several hotels. When he passed through the lobby several of the loungers there gave him an odd glance. The Sloan was not among the better hotels in the mining town, and a man dressed as handsomely—and as expensively—as LeFarge would not be expected to have rooms there.

LeFarge ignored the men in the lobby and continued on up the narrow staircase like a man who knew where he was going. He reached the third, and top, floor of the hotel and walked quickly down the corridor to the third room on the left. He opened the door and went inside without knocking.

"Good. I was afraid you might be out," he said.

Two people shared the sweaty, rumpled bed in the dingy little hotel room.

One was a large man, dark-haired and full-bearded. The

man was half a head taller than LeFarge and probably out-
weighed him by seventy pounds, all of it hard slabs of
muscle. In spite of his size and the bearlike appearance he
must have had when dressed, his now naked body was
almost hairless. Oiled and gleaming with a sheen of sweat,
the big man's muscles rippled when he twisted to see who
had caused the interruption.

His companion in the bed was considerably smaller but
equally naked. She was young, but her body was already
flaccid and bruised from hard and probably professional use.
Her skin was dark and her eyes black, but her hair had been
artificially lightened to a copper-blond shade that was lu-
dicrous in combination with her dark, Hispanic features.
Her cheeks and lips had been stained with artless applica-
tions of some carmine tint. LeFarge paused for a moment
and reflected that she might have been one of the homeliest
women he had ever seen. Which could almost be classified
as an accomplishment. There were times, LeFarge thought,
when he definitely had to question Rolf's tastes.

Neither Rolf nor the woman seemed in the least concerned about their nakedness in front of LeFarge.

Rolf had been mounting the whore from behind when
LeFarge came in. The coupling was much like that of a
stallion covering a seasoned mare.

Now Rolf pulled away from the woman and sat on the
edge of the none-too-clean bed, his erection slowly receding
as he reached for a cigar and box of matches on the night
table nearby. The woman rolled over onto her back and
waited patiently for whatever might happen next. Her breasts
were small and wrinkled, and her nipples had been rouged
with the same material that discolored her cheeks.

In spite of her ugliness, her frank, functional availability,
the shine of sweat rubbed onto her body by another man's
lust, brought a surge of arousal into LeFarge's crotch. Her
attitude of total acceptance seemed to imply that anything
that might be done to her now would already be known and
normal. Anything.

LeFarge forced his eyes away from the patch of bleached

hair at the whore's pubis and looked at Rolf, who had his cigar lighted now and was waiting for LeFarge to speak again.

"Are you going to need her very long?" LeFarge asked. It was not what he had come here to say.

Rolf smiled. "Yah. Gave her ten dollar, boss. She know she gonna be hurtin' when she leave here. Gonna have me a big time with this 'un."

"If she can still walk when you're done with her, send her over to my place."

The big man's smile grew wider. "She won' walk, but I carry her, eh?"

LeFarge nodded. To the whore he said, "You need to visit the *pissoir* now. Ten, fifteen minutes. Then come back."

"The pisser," Rolf explained. "Go down the hall, take a leak. Come back half hour." When she was not quick to come to her feet, Rolf pushed her off the bed. She moved more quickly after that, pulling on a short dress and hurrying out into the hallway.

LeFarge noted that even though she must have been in pain she had made no sound and offered no protest to the treatment. He was already beginning to think of ways he could enjoy her when Rolf was through with her.

"Now," he said as soon as the door was closed and he and Rolf were alone in the cheap hotel room. "I have some work for you that won't wait. Come to think of it, this might take a while. I'll go ahead and take her with me. You can find yourself another one when you're done."

Rolf nodded. He seemed to take no exception to LeFarge's decision. But then, one whore was much the same as any other.

"Have you ever heard of a Pinkerton man named Raider?"

Rolf's expression, calm and accepting till now, hardened into a rigid mask of controlled hatred. "Yah, boss. That sumbitch, he killed some friends of mine. When I find that Raider, boss, I kill him good. It's gonna take him all fuckin' day to die, you bet."

*"Merde,"* LeFarge muttered.

"Huh?"

"We have some business with this Raider, Rolf, but you can't kill him. Not for a while. Do you understand that?"

Rolf did not say anything at once. LeFarge repeated the question.

"Yah, boss. I understand."

"Good. That is important, Rolf. Extremely important. I will give him to you later, but for now it is important that Mr. Raider remain alive."

Rolf looked confused.

"This former Pinkerton man is going to be of great help to us, Rolf." LeFarge helped himself to one of Rolf's cigars and lighted it. He laughed. "With luck, my dear man, it may even be possible for you to collect a reward from the law when you are given permission to kill Raider."

Rolf definitely looked confused now.

"Temptations, Rolf. We are all subject to them." LeFarge laughed again. "As you and I know quite well, eh? Yes, we understand about temptations. This Raider of yours was tempted once too often, it seems. The Pinkerton Agency is keeping it all very hush-hush." He smiled. "Professional embarrassment and all that. But it seems that one of their own people, Raider in fact, jumped over the line and turned on them. You are going to love this one, Rolf. When Raider went over to the easy side of the law, it was the damned Pinkertons' own payroll that he stole. I almost admire him for that, actually. A truly lovely touch, that."

LeFarge began to pace about the small room, gesturing with the cigar. Sage pontification was something he enjoyed, and Rolf was always an attentive audience.

"It is quite true, Rolf. Raider made off with the Pinkertons' own payroll. And now, without explaining their reasons, they are making carefully quiet inquiries of law enforcement agencies throughout the country and in particular in the border communities requesting the apprehension of their former agent." LeFarge chuckled. "Delightful, no?"

Rolf shrugged. "So why can't I kill 'im?"

"A logical question, my dear fellow, but you see, before Raider seized his opportunity for instant wealth, he had been assigned to the protection of the gold shipment scheduled later this month from Leadville to San Francisco."

Gold shipments in this day and age were a rarity from Leadville. In its early days, before and during the Civil War, Leadville had been a gold mining camp. Then the shipments were frequent. It was only later, when the gold was playing out and the high, remote camp was dying, that someone discovered that the blue mud that had been mucking up the ore separators for years was a highly concentrated silver ore.

Leadville had experienced its second boom then, and a more lasting one. Now it was almost exclusively a silver mining town and one that had achieved a remarkable degree of permanence.

Now it was silver that was frequently shipped by rail for sale at the United States mint in Denver.

Silver shipments, however, were as good as safe from robbery. The sheer bulk of poorly concentrated raw silver made it impractical for anyone to steal a silver shipment.

Gold, however, was another story. There was still some of it mined in Leadville, largely as a by-product of the silver production. Because the gold was so much more valuable than the silver and in so much more easily manageable a load, the mine operators stockpiled their gold and shipped it infrequently to the much larger San Francisco mint under heavy guard.

This shipment would be an exceptionally large one. The last scheduled movement of gold from Leadville had been postponed twice, first by a snow blockage on the rails below Leadville in the Arkansas Valley, then again by a bridge washout during the spring melt. Now the mines intended to take out what amounted to virtually a double shipment of the gold they had been accumulating since last fall.

It was Charles LeFarge's intention to divert that gold shipment into his own hands.

And the ex-Pinkerton man Raider had been involved in

the planning stages of the protection for that shipment.

Good as LeFarge's sources of information were, they could not match that kind of intimate knowledge.

It was this that he now explained to Rolf.

"The thing is," LeFarge continued, "Raider is almost certainly here with the intention of stealing that gold."

"Let me kill him. He won't steal no gold then," Rolf said.

"Nor would he be able to help us if you kill him before we take the shipment," LeFarge said. "No, my good man. First we enlist Mr. Raider's assistance in our venture. Then you kill him."

Rolf grunted. It was as close to active disagreement as he was likely to express. Over the years they had been working together, Rolf had learned to trust Charles LeFarge. That was something he would have been able to say of no other man.

"Raider is in Leadville in disguise, of course." LeFarge went on. "He calls himself Jason Jones, and he has money to spend. I ran into him at the White Owl tonight. Played cards with him, in fact. He would have no way to know who I am, but I recognized him in spite of his attempts at disguise."

"However, my dear Rolf, as long as Mr. Raider is in a position to act independently, he will have no need of a partnership with us. Our next move must be to modify that condition."

Rolf looked confused.

LeFarge smiled. "I shall tell you exactly what to do, of course."

"Yah, but I druther kill him."

"Soon enough, Rolf. I promise. Raider's life shall be my little gift to you as quickly as we have no further need for him."

Rolf looked pleased.

"Listen closely now while I tell you what must be done tonight."

A few minutes later Rolf nodded and stood. "I won't kill him. Not tonight," he promised.

"Good man," LeFarge said. He reached into his pocket and pulled out three double eagles. "When you are done," he said, "get yourselves some women. My treat."

Rolf grinned and accepted the coins. Twenty dollars would buy him total obedience for as long as any woman was likely to last.

"Now if you would please call the young, uh, lady back into the room?"

Rolf was still naked, but he either did not care or did not bother to notice. He walked out into the hall and down to the end of the corridor to where the Mexican whore was waiting huddled in the hotel's crude bathing room. He moved with the flowing, unconscious grace of a catamount, muscles rippling in the lamplight with every fluid motion.

Charles LeFarge could remember his father, in long ago and much better times, once owning a mastiff with the same degree of raw power and unquestioning loyalty. The elder LeFarge had always treated the dog with deep affection. Charles felt much the same way toward Rolf now.

Rolf returned with the woman moments later. LeFarge gave her a moment to gather up her shoes and stockings and smallclothes, then offered her his elbow to escort her to his own hotel room, which was much better than any the Sloan House could boast.

The whore seemed surprised by the gesture. LeFarge did it quite naturally, as if it were correct and proper to treat a street whore with the same respect generally accorded to a lady.

She was smiling when he led her out into the night.

But then she probably had no idea that Charles LeFarge was thinking with growing excitement about the riding crop that now lay waiting in the wardrobe in his room and about the tiny, mother-of-pearl-handled penknife that was in his pocket.

Charles LeFarge was looking forward to a most memorable evening.

# CHAPTER FOUR

Raider looked at Marcia. He did not like having to trust her to keep her mouth shut, but it was necessary if he and Doc were to be able to meet. Leadville was small, and it was crowded. The chances of being seen if they met in any public place were just too great, Raider's frequent partnership with Doc Weatherbee was entirely too well known, and Charles LeFarge's sources of information were apparently too good for them to take any risks.

Yet they were taking a chance by trusting Marcia to remain quiet. At least they had the railroad's hold over her boyfriend to help keep her in line. If Raider and Doc reported back favorably on her help, the railroad had promised not to press legal charges against Jack Cawthon. The man was in jail now facing certain conviction for a passenger car holdup that went wrong.

23

Raider understood—although he had not been the one to deliver the message himself when her help was recruited—that it had been impressed on the girl that it would be his report and Doc's that would determine whether Cawthon went to trial or was released.

Pressure like that gave him more power over her than Raider really wanted. Yet it had seemed necessary—and still did.

If she talked, the very least that would happen would be that their mission would be destroyed. It could well become much worse than that. LeFarge, despite his refinement and manners, was not above ordering a killing. And no one, no matter how good he is, is immune from ambush. Not Raider, not Doc, no one.

Raider looked at her now, then turned to lock the window and swing the shutters back in place the way he had found them earlier.

"Raider?" The girl got off the bed and began to come to him.

"Jason," he corrected. "You got to remember that I'm Jason Jones. You can't know me by any other name here. I'm sorry my friend told you any different, but it's too late to take it back now."

"All right. Jason. You're sure they'll let my Jackie outta jail when this is done?"

"It isn't up to me, but that's the deal."

"An' they can do it? That's the truth?"

"Oh, that's true enough. All the railroad has to do to spring him is tell the prosecutor they aren't gonna press the charges. If they say that, there won't be no case against him."

"What about them federal people? I understand they ain't so easy to get along with."

She was right, but for a moment Raider wondered where she might have come by knowledge like that. Then he realized that this young and reasonably pretty little Leadville whore would have been a party to experiences and conversations that might surprise even him. It was hard telling what kind of men she might have been keeping company with in her line of work. Railroad robbers might be the least of it.

"The feds aren't involved," he explained. "I don't know that they would have been willing to make any deals, but your boyfriend wasn't anywhere near the mail car when he pulled his iron and tried to get rich the easy way. He was taking down the passengers when that conductor slipped up behind and bashed him. That's plain old armed robbery. State offense, not federal. An' they're willing to deal if the big boys at the railroad want them to."

Marcia sighed. She thought it over for a moment, then nodded. "All right then."

Raider headed for the door, but she stepped in front of him to block his exit.

"Something you want?"

Her answer was to put her arms around his waist and nuzzle against his chest. She was making soft, cooing sounds and wriggling herself against his pelvis.

Raider responded as any man would. The contact, the completely obvious offer, aroused him and sent his cock pulsing against the restrictions of his buttoned fly.

"Look, Marcia, you don't have to—"

"Shhhh." She pressed a fingertip to his lips to silence him, then stepped back just long enough to drop her dress from her shoulders and skinny out of it. She wore nothing else but her shoes and black cotton stockings attached to a garter belt.

Her breasts sagged, but from the waist down she somehow managed to retain a ghost of youth. Her belly was flat and her thighs still slim. Her pubic hair was short and curly. He wondered if she trimmed it to keep it that way.

"I thought you were in love with this Jackie."

"What's that got to do with anything?" She smiled and added, "Jason."

"Why this then?" Raider was far from being uninterested in the offer she was making. But he had already told her she could keep the money he had paid her. And he didn't like being used unless he knew the reason why. He had to ask the question.

"I like you, Jason." She reached out to caress him through the barrier of the cloth, then dropped to her knees in front of him and began undoing the buttons at his fly. "You're so handsome an' fine lookin'. I just want you."

Raider laughed. He began to lose his erection. "Honey," he said, "I might not be the brightest feller there is in the woods, but I know better'n that. You do this for a livin', not for fun."

Marcia looked up at him and made a face. Then she grinned, and she too began to laugh. "All right, Jason, but it goes against my grain t' tell you the truth."

"Which is?"

"If you just got to know, honey, I wanna make sure you're in my corner when this crap is all done with."

"Like I said, Marcia, it's the railroad that will make that decision, not me."

"I know, but I want you on my side. I mean, it ain't like I'm offering you some big deal that half the sons o' bitches in Leadville haven't already had." She winked at him. "An' I am pretty good, if I do say so myself." She reached for him again and resumed the task of flipping buttons out of their holes.

Raider looked down at her. A toothsome morsel, LeFarge had called her. He had been right.

She finished what she was doing and reached inside his trousers to pull him free.

He was fully erect again now.

"I don't s'pose you'll believe me now," she said, "but you really are hung right, aren't you?"

Raider said nothing. It was just a whore's bullshit, he told himself.

Still, he didn't try again to stop her.

She ran her fingers up and down the length of him and followed that touch with light, swift flickerings of her tongue.

She had told him the truth about one thing, he decided. She was good at what she did.

She stayed with him only long enough to tease, then pulled away and drew him over to the bed where she helped him off with his clothing. Raider handled his gunbelt himself, hanging it at the head of the bed where he could get to it if he had to. There was no woman he would trust completely with his safety.

"Lay down an' roll onto your stomach, Jason," she directed.

That was something that he would trust to a woman. He did as she asked.

Marcia knelt over him. Her hair, brown and curly, was pinned high in the current fashion. He watched as she removed the pins and let her hair cascade down over her shoulders and breasts.

She leaned forward and began to sway from side to side. The gently curling ends of her hair trailed lightly, teasingly across his flesh.

Her head dropped lower, and now it was her tongue that was tantalizing him.

She took her time, licking and nibbling across his shoulders and down his back, concentrating along his spine and then down to his ass. The sensation was remarkable.

She continued still lower, down his legs and to his feet. Slowly, one by one, she took his toes into her mouth, sucking each one separately with much care.

When she was done with each toe, her tongue darted into the crevices between them before she took the next into her mouth.

Finally she touched him with her hands, silently asking him to roll onto his back. Again he did as instructed.

Marcia began to work her way back up, more quickly this time. One glance would have made it obvious that he was as completely aroused as it was possible for a man to get. His cock had taken on the texture of marble from the constant and seductive ministrations she was giving him.

She burrowed her face between his legs, forcing his thighs wide, and drew first one engorged ball and then the other gently into her mouth. Her breath was hot, and his need was becoming painful. The very slightest touch now was searing overly sensitized nerve endings.

With a faint moan of anticipation—or perhaps it was he who had made the sound, he was not really sure—Marcia ran her tongue over the head of his cock and then lowered herself onto it, engulfing him deep inside her mouth and sucking him hard.

Raider's hips rose involuntarily to meet her.

Still applying the strong suction, she pulled away from him. There was a loud, wet, plopping noise as she pulled herself away against the tug of the suction. She laughed, pleased with herself.

Well, that was reasonable. Raider was pleased with her too.

"This way, honey?" she asked. "Or would you like it someplace else?" She smiled at him and dropped her head to give him a light kiss on the tip end of his cock.

Raider groaned. The hell with taking the time to change positions and start something new. He cupped the back of her head in his hand and pressed her face down onto him.

Chuckling, as if she had already known what he would decide, Marcia wet her lips and then attacked him with renewed vigor.

Saliva lubricated him and eased his passage deep into her throat. Much deeper than he had thought it possible for a woman to accept a man.

She gagged once but did not withdraw. She pressed harder against him, and he could feel a restrictive ring of cartilage at the opening to her throat. Then the head of his cock slipped through and beyond the restriction, and he was fully inside her there.

Even then she had more to give. While she held him there, she reached down to cup his balls and lightly caress them with soft fingertips.

Raider felt as if all of him, every last scrap of his manhood, was being warmed and suckled and surrounded.

He groaned again, and Marcia bobbed her head up and down with quick, short strokes. Fingers, lips, and throat constricted all at the same time, and Raider felt himself reaching a climax that had an intensity beyond belief.

Hot, sticky fluid spewed out of him in a torrent.

Marcia clamped her lips tight around the base of his cock, slowing the flow and making it last for an unnaturally long time. The pressure seemed to heighten the pleasure he was receiving as well as prolonging it.

Raider cried out into the silence of the room.

He relaxed and was embarrassed to discover that he was still pressing harshly down on the back of her head, pinning her there with his now emptied tool still trapped deep in her mouth.

A chill ran up his spine in the aftermath of such intense pleasure, and he shook his shoulders, allowing his hand finally to drop away. He let it trail down the back of her neck and petted her shoulder.

Only then did Marcia release her hold on him and allow him to slip free of her as she raised her head and turned to smile at him.

"Damn," he said. There was a tone in his voice that was close to disbelieving awe.

She laughed again. Apparently the tone of voice had been enough to show his appreciation. "You're welcome, Jason."

She gave him another brief kiss, and the tip of her tongue darted out to lick up a final droplet of sperm that had appeared at the tiny hole in the end of his cock.

"You were right," he said.

"About what, honey?"

"About being so damned good."

She smiled but did not otherwise respond to the compliment. Apparently she knew how very good she was.

"Not just everybody gets that," she said. "And you better believe it."

He laughed with pleasure—he did believe it, as a matter of fact—and ran his thumb along the angle of her jaw.

Something else bumped against the underside of her jaw, and she looked down. "Hey now," she said with surprise. "It sure hell ain't everybody that can come back so soon from what I jus' gave you, honey. What this time?"

His answer was to pull her down beside him.

Marcia lay on her back and reached for him.

It was all the encouragement Raider needed. He rolled onto her and let her guide the way.

# CHAPTER FIVE

Doc climbed carefully onto the roof, hampered both by the sheer bulk of his padding and by the fact that he didn't want to disarrange the carefully planned disguise. After all, it would be hard to be taken seriously as a fat old drunk if his stomach suddenly shifted under his left armpit.

He padded silently across the roof toward the left side of the building, fretting as he walked. He had had to leave Judith in the care of a public livery back in Denver, and for the moment his thoughts were occupied by concern for the mule. He genuinely liked the animal, but he had used her too many times in the past to risk his medicine show disguise again here. Charles LeFarge's sources of information—and wouldn't it be a feather in their cap if they could determine what *those* were as well as stopping LeFarge?— were just too consistently good to repeat that trick now. Meanwhile he had to wonder and worry about

31

the care Judith was getting from strangers.

There was no fire escape or any other planned way to reach the roof of the saloon building, but earlier Doc had found a set of spikes, probably left there by some workmen—or perhaps by some foresighted burglar—in the past. The well-driven spikes provided a ladder of sorts up the left, or southern, wall of the building. It was those that had given Doc access to the roof and to Marcia's bedroom for the meeting with Raider.

The roof had been constructed flat—surprising to Doc in area known for its exceptionally heavy winter snows—and covered with black tar for protection against the hostile elements. A tall, false front concealed any rooftop activity from observers in the buildings across the street. The tar was hard and probably brittle in the chill of the night air, but still it offered enough padding underfoot that Doc had no great difficulty crossing it without sound.

He reached the far edge and knelt to find his footholds for the drop down to ground level.

Then he cursed under his breath and scuttled cautiously back away from the edge.

In the narrow alley down below he could see movement in the dim light from the nearby street.

Doc lay flat on the roof, took off his hat, and set it aside. If someone was really down there it wouldn't be advisable to drop things onto them. He peered over the rim and cursed a little more.

There were two men in the alley. What they might be doing there he could not immediately guess. The thought of thugs waiting to waylay some well-heeled passerby came to mind, but several men, including one who was quite well dressed, crossed the mouth of the alley without either of the waiting men reacting in the slightest.

Whatever their reason, as long as they chose to remain in the alley Doc was trapped on the roof above them. He couldn't risk being seen coming or going by this access route. Not if he intended to use it again for his meetings with Raider. Or Jason Jones.

While Doc watched, one of the men pulled tobacco and

papers from his pocket and rolled himself a smoke after first offering his makings to his companion. The flare of a match illuminated the men's coats, but from his position above them all Doc could see was the unlighted silhouettes of their hat brims.

The one with the cigarette kept the match aflame long enough to find a discarded crate in the litter that nearly filled the alley. The man upended the crate and sat on it, leaning back against the wall and crossing his legs.

Doc cussed some more to himself. It looked like they were settling in there for a wait. And Doc would have to wait just as long before he could come down off the rooftop.

The thought of a smoke seemed a good one, so Doc backed slowly away from the edge of the roof, then came to his feet. He padded softly away, not wanting to take any chance on being seen there, and took shelter behind the framed woodwork of the saloon's false front. He pulled an old Virginia cheroot from under his padding—an aging drunk would not be expected to carry a decent smoke— and bent low to light it with his match cupped between his hands.

He took his time enjoying the smoke, then drifted silently back to the edge of the roof. The men were still there, still waiting. Doc returned to the false front and leaned against it.

Idly, he peered over the lower, side section of the false front and looked down into the street. There were no lights above or behind him that could give him away there. Down at the street level there was little enough light coming through the windows of the saloons and hotels and closed stores along Leadville's main street.

There was a hotel across the way. It had no porch or veranda to speak of, but a man sat in front of the place on the steps leading up to the hotel lobby. The man sat bent forward, holding something cupped in his hands. He seemed to be watching the entrance to the building where Doc was now patiently waiting. And from time to time the man looked toward the mouth of the alley where the others waited too.

Odd, Doc thought. He tried to see what the fellow was holding. A weapon? But there was too little light and the distance was too far.

People, most of them men dressed in the rough work clothing of underground miners, passed on the far side of the street, and Doc could hear footsteps on the board walkway below. But the traffic was thinning now as the evening lengthened into early morning. Still the men in the alley and the one sitting in front of the hotel sat and waited.

He heard laughter below, and the man in front of the hotel came to sharp attention. Then relaxed. Doc heard footsteps receding down the street as a party of late-night revelers trooped home. Doc wished he could do the same.

The sound of those footsteps faded. Moments later Doc could hear booted heels strike the boards in front of the saloon. One man, it sounded like.

Again the hotel watcher's head tilted slightly. This time he moved.

It was not a weapon he had been holding cupped in his hands all this time but a pipe and match. He put the stem of the pipe between his teeth and scratched the match aflame on the rough wood of the hotel steps, then quickly rose and disappeared inside the hotel lobby.

A signal, Doc realized. The flame of the match would easily been seen from inside the alley.

His curiosity piqued now, Doc hurried across the roof to see what the men in the alley were doing.

He had been right that it was a signal they had been given. The men were near the mouth of the alley now, their backs pressed flat against the wall of the saloon.

If it wouldn't have meant giving himself away, Doc would have shouted a warning out of sheer contrariness, whoever it was the trio had been laying for.

A figure he recognized entirely too well stepped off the saloon boardwalk before the mouth of the narrow alley, and Doc had to clamp his jaws shut to keep from crying out.

Raider!

It was tall, well-dressed Raider they were waiting for.

While Doc watched, helpless because of more than just the distance involved, one of the men—a very large man, Doc could see now that he had Raider's own lean height for comparison—clubbed Raider from behind with practiced skill.

Raider's leg buckled, and he was undoubtedly disoriented by the unexpected blow on the back of his skull.

A blow like that could easily kill a man, and swift anger sent Doc's hand leaping for the .38 revolver at his waist. For the moment he had forgotten that the revolver, like his cigars, had to be hidden beneath layers of cotton padding. He could get to it, but not quickly.

Son of a bitch, Doc thought, his normal calm disrupted.

Raider staggered, and the two thugs stepped out of their hiding place only long enough to grab him under the arms and hustle him into the dark shelter of the alley. The time was too short and the light too poor for Doc to get a good look at them. The big man was bearded. He was sure of that but of nothing more.

If they intended to kill Raider...

Doc's hand clawed at the buttons of his shirt as he frantically hunted for the butt of the revolver he could feel against his stomach but could not reach.

The smaller of the two held Raider while the big one shifted around in front of Doc's defenseless partner.

Raider was wobbling, too stunned to make a fight of it. Doc cursed some more and ripped his disguise into complete disarray, but the compact Colt still eluded him.

Down below, the big man hooked a hard punch into Raider's stomach. The blow was powerful. Doc could almost feel it himself.

Raider doubled forward against the restraint of the other man's hold. He retched, and a stream of puke and bile arched forward to splatter the big man's trousers and shoes.

Doc finally found the grips of his Colt and pulled the gun free of the padding. He aimed it.

But, damnit, the two men had no weapons. There was no glint of lamplight on steel, no sign of knife or gun.

If Doc fired it would save Raider from a beating and robbery. It would also destroy their so carefully conceived cover here.

Shaking with frustration and anger, Doc forced himself to withhold his fire.

If they tried to kill Raider...

But they did not.

Obviously furious now about the soiling of his clothing, the big man battered Raider with one punch after another. The bruising would be deep and slow to heal. But the beating would not be fatal.

Doc took careful aim in the uncertain light. He lined his sights on the torso of the big man who was delivering the beating. He could not bring himself to fire. He could not. Not unless or until he had to to preserve Raider's life.

Raider must have lost consciousness. He slumped forward, his knees giving way completely, and the man who was holding him lost his grip and let Raider fall into the slime of his own vomit.

Doc thumbed back the hammer of the Colt. The .38 was a double-action revolver, but the trigger pull would be lighter and the shot more truly aimed if it was already cocked like a single action of the antiquated type that Raider preferred.

The smaller man delivered a kick to Raider's kidneys, then both of them knelt and quickly frisked through Raider's pockets.

Robbery then, not murder, Doc thought.

He bit his lip and held in the scream of rage he felt trying to well out of him. He also lowered the hammer of the .38.

The thugs made quick work of their theft, then came to their feet. The big one kicked Raider again, the toe of his shoe gouging into Raider's stomach.

Then the two turned and ran.

Bastards, Doc silently thought behind them.

Doc returned the Colt to its hiding place and began trying to repair his disguise.

Down below there was enough light reaching the front portion of the alley for him to see Raider move. Very slowly and very little at first, but he was moving.

Raider got his hands under him and levered his chest off the ground. Then came to his knees.

He shook his head and vomited again.

He hung there, head drooping, on hands and knees, for several moments. Then he came staggering to his feet and leaned against the wall for support. He was holding his stomach and was hurting, but he was alive and on his feet. Even so, Doc had to stifle an impulse to race down the ladder of spikes to lend aid and comfort.

But to do that now would be to risk destroying everything they had planned here. And Raider had already suffered the worst of it.

With a sigh of raw frustration, Doc Weatherbee stepped back from the edge of the roof and gave his attention to his disguise.

The next time he looked down into the alley it was empty. Raider was gone.

Doc cussed some more, then silently climbed down into the alley.

He made his way out through the back of the alley, avoiding the public streets, and went back to the temporary quarters he had established for himself in his role as a derelict: a derailed and overturned boxcar at the edge of the town. That choice had been a deliberate one, giving him no comfort and scant guarantee of privacy but fitting in with his disguise and at the same time giving him access to the trains if he needed to travel down to Buena Vista so he could communicate with the agency or with their employer on this special assignment.

He made it back without being seen, as far as he knew, but under the circumstances that gave him small comfort.

He was no longer as sure as he had been that this job was going to come off as they had planned.

# CHAPTER SIX

Whatever had brought him here, Raider was no longer sure. Whether it was some instinctive, searching need or simply that this was the nearest possible haven, closer than his room down at the Grand Paree, he really did not know.

Whatever it had been, he slumped against the closed door to Marcia's bedroom and knocked feebly on the wooden panel.

He could barely remember crossing the saloon floor below. Customers had turned to stare, but none had offered help.

He remembered all too well the struggle to get up— crawl up—the stairs.

Now his strength was exhausted. He had completely used up what little there had been after the beating.

His gut hurt, his head ached horribly, and his thoughts were floating loosely in a hazy fog.

If the woman turned him away now, he would just have to lie in the damned hallway until he felt well enough to drag himself back to his room. *If* he could drag himself that far. The Grand Paree was two blocks away.

He tapped on the door again, and Marcia opened it.

Raider had not thought about that. He had been bracing himself against the door, not the jamb. As soon as she released the latch his weight pushed the door open, and he tumbled to the floor half inside her room and half out in the hallway.

"Ra . . . Jason!"

He lay there blinking up at her.

"Here. Help me get him onto the bed." There was a short pause. "Please, damn it. Help me."

Raider felt hands taking hold of him under the arms and lifting. He was conscious enough to be surprised by the girl's strength. Then he realized that it was a man's face hovering over him as he was lifted and dragged toward the bed.

Another set of hands lifted his feet, and he felt himself being placed onto the soft comfort of the whore's rumpled bed, still sweaty from his own recent exertions there. He remembered the smell of those sheets.

"I'm sorry as hell, mister," Marcia was saying. "Look, I'll give you your money back. Okay? An' tomorra you come back an' you can have a free fuck. How's that? Get yourself another girl tonight. A fine-lookin' gentleman like you won't have no trouble finding another girl downstairs. An' tomorra, you and me will have us a party. No charge. Okay?"

"French too?" a man's voice asked.

"Sure, honey." Pause. "I don't go in for that sorta thing usually, but with you, honey, it'll be a pleasure."

"No charge?" The man sounded grumpy but interested.

"My word on it, honey. Soon as you get off shift tommorra, you come in an' little Marcia will drain all you got." She laughed. "I'll do you so good, honey, you won't need any for the next month."

"All right then."

There was a sound of footsteps and the closing of a door.

He heard the metallic snick of a bolt being thrown and then Marcia was beside him. "What the fuck happened to you?"

Raider opened his eyes. He did not remember having closed them. The woman was sitting on the edge of the bed beside him. She was naked and must have been interrupted in mid hump. He hadn't thought he'd been gone long enough for her to find another customer.

On the other hand, he wasn't really sure how much time might have passed between his leaving and his return. It could have been a great deal more than he realized.

He sighed, and she began undoing his buttons.

She made a face. "Honey, you stink."

"Thanks." The single word came out as something closer to a croak than a human voice, but he did get it out. That seemed like something of an accomplishment.

He could smell it too now that she reminded him of it. His clothes carried the sour odor of puke. Becoming aware of the smell made him want to puke again, and he had to fight to hold it back.

Marcia stripped him and held the bundle of fouled clothing away from her.

She dropped Raider's clothes on the floor and went to a hook on the far wall—there were no such conveniences in the room as even a wardrobe—for a kimono that she pulled on and belted shut.

"I'll be right back," she said. She picked up his clothes and left the room.

"Hey!" Raider protested, but she was already gone.

When she returned—quickly, he thought, although he was still fuzzy when it came to the passage of time—there was no sign of the clothing she had taken away, and she was carrying a basin of water and a small pile of towels.

She locked the door behind her and set the basin and towels on the floor beside the bed. She dipped one of the towels into the water and wrung it partially dry again, then began to bathe Raider's aching body.

The water was warm and soothing, he discovered. Her touch was firm and competent.

"You—" He choked and had to try again before he could make the words come. "You do that pretty good."

She shrugged and continued to work on him. "Lots of practice," she said. "I had a bunch of damn brothers. They were brawlin' sons o' bitches, all of them."

Raider nodded. The movement hurt, and he winced at the pain.

Marcia felt lightly at the back of his head and reported, "You have one hell of a goose egg back there, but there's no blood. Musta been wearing your hat."

"I guess so. Where is it?"

"Where's what?" She wiped his face. A split at the corner of his mouth stung, but she was gentle about it.

"Hat. Where's my hat?"

"Damned if I know. You wasn't wearing one when you dropped in." She smiled at the small joke she had made, and he surprised himself by feeling up to smiling with her.

"Shit," he said. "Where's my gun?" He couldn't remember seeing her pick up his gunbelt when she gathered his clothing.

"You ain't got one of them neither," Marcia told him.

"Bitch," he said.

"Me?"

"Life."

"Yeah, ain't that the truth." The warmth of the towel moved down over his chest and across his belly. The heat felt good there. Soothing. He could feel the pain-taut muscles begin to relax.

While she was at it, she continued lower and washed his privates of the juices she herself had helped him deposit there a short while earlier.

"There's a bruise on your belly," she observed.

"That's the worst," he said.

She wet the towel in the warm water again and wrung it, then draped it over his stomach to let the heat do its work of revival. Then she got a dry towel and began drying the rest of his body.

"You shoulda been a nurse," he said.

She laughed, but there was no humor in the sound. It was short and sharp and bitter.

Raider touched her hand by way of apology.

A wave of pain racked through him, and he closed his eyes. She reached across him for the thin, flat pillow that had been wedged between the bed and the wall during her most recent visitor's activities. Very gently she plumped it up and slipped it behind his neck. He opened his eyes. "Thanks."

She shrugged.

"I really ought to get out of your way here," he said.

"You ain't in any shape to be taking a stroll."

"But..."

"Besides," she went on, ignoring him, "you can't go around bare-assed. Folks would talk."

He tried to struggle into a sitting position, but she calmed him quickly. "Your things will be back by morning," she said. "We got a lot of laundry to do here, y'know. Sheets an' towels an' such. Got a niggra woman that keeps 'em done up. She'll have everything back by dawn or a little after. You can stay here till then."

"Thanks," he said again. He smiled. "Looks like I got a bunch to thank you for, dosen't it?"

She smiled. "I did say that I wanted you on my side when this was over. It don't hurt if you think you owe me."

"Fair enough," Raider said. "I think I owe you."

"Good." She removed the cooling towel from his belly and leaned down to feel of the water left in the basin. "This ain't warm enough to do you any good now," she said. She dried his stomach, then gathered up the towels and the basin and carried them to the small table beside the window.

"Anything more you want?" she asked.

"A drink would be nice, if it isn't too much trouble. You can take the money out of my pa..." He stopped. He didn't have any pants for her to take the money from.

Marcia laughed. "Honey, you don't have any money, if that's where you was keeping it. You been picked clean as a flat rock in a creek bed."

"Shit," Raider mumbled.

But at least that gave him some hope that the beating was unrelated to his assignment here. It could well have been dumb, lousy chance that had made the robbers choose him when he came out of the saloon. He had been halfway thinking that he was an intentional target and that perhaps his cover had been blown in spite of all the precautions they had taken to get him here and into position.

That, he reminded himself, was the big thing. He had come here to get a job done. That much had not changed.

"Get yourself some sleep, honey," Marcia said.

"What about you?"

"Too early to quit for the night, honey. I got a girlfriend that's taking a few days off with the vapors." She laughed. "I'll go see if I can use her room the rest o' the night. I'll come back an' check on you when the customers slack off."

Raider nodded.

Marcia replaced the kimono on the wall hook and stepped into her dress. She let herself out quietly.

Raider listened for the click of a lock being turned, but there was none. He felt vulnerable with no revolver and no lock on the door, but he wasn't up to doing anything about it.

He closed his eyes and let the healing relief of sleep take him out of the pain that still lay just under the surface of his battered muscles.

Raider was dreaming. He could feel warmth against him. It felt good.

He opened his eyes to darkness, but he could still feel the warmth. His head was aching but not very badly.

"Sorry if I woke you." It was Marcia's voice. She was in the bed at his side, although there wasn't really room enough for two people to sleep there comfortably.

"What time is it?"

"Coming dawn soon," she whispered.

She smelled clean, as if she had just come from a bath, and there was an artificial, flowery scent on her skin in addition to that of soap and clean woman-smell.

Raider felt considerably better than he had. That was perfectly obvious from his reaction to the presence of the woman whose body was pressed against his.

Her nearness, enforced by the size of the bed, made her instantly aware of his changed condition. He heard a low chuckle close to his left ear, and she said, "I shouldn't oughta be surprised by any damn thing a man does, honey, but you sure can surprise a lady."

"Sorry."

"Hell, I don't mind." Her hand moved to grasp and stroke him, although it was encouragement that he didn't really need. He was already hard and willing. Marcia chuckled again.

"Scootch over an' give me room to lay flat," she said.

Raider tried, but the movement was painful. She must have heard or sensed the sharp intake of breath because she said, "It's all right, honey. Lay still. I'll take care of it."

"All right." He didn't protest. The pain had subsided and was just fine as long as he lay still, but there was plenty of it still around and waiting to be found when he moved.

He felt her stir on the bed beside him, and then there was the feather-light touch of her hair sliding softly over his stomach.

A moment more and he could feel himself being engulfed in the moist heat of her mouth.

Raider relaxed and let himself drift with the flow of the sensations she was giving him.

His muscles tightened only once, but by then it was too late for the pain to distract him.

The flow of pleasure was swift and relaxing. He let it slide, eyes still closed and all thoughts of pain gone from his mind.

Sleep reclaimed him. The last thing he remembered was Marcia's low, soft chuckle in the night.

# CHAPTER SEVEN

Raider had no idea what time it was when he woke up the second time, but the heat in the room coming through the uninsulated ceiling was enough to tell him it was well past dawn. The shuttered windows, though, kept Marcia's room in almost total darkness. He eased off the bed and across the sleeping woman, pleased that he was able to do so without a great deal of pain. Even his headache had settled to a dull, hardly noticeable throbbing. The rest had done him good.

He padded across the floor and opened the shutters. The sky was lightly overcast, but he could see that it was nearly noon. He rubbed at his eyes and ran a hand across the unfamiliar fur of the beard he had grown as part of the "disguise" that was not really supposed to disguise him from LeFarge. Everything depended on LeFarge recognizing him.

When he turned from the window, Marcia was propped up on one elbow, sleepily looking at him.

"Good morning," he said.

"You look like you feel better today."

He smiled. "Thanks to you."

"Just don't forget it when it comes time to get my Jackie outta that pisshole downcountry."

"I won't." It still amazed Raider that the woman would so freely and fully participate in virtually any sexual activity, with virtually any sexual partner, and still claim to be so interested in her fiancé's future. But then, the older he got, the less he thought he knew about human behavior.

"I'll get your clothes for you if you want."

"Thanks."

She didn't have far to go. Raider's things, looking and smelling infinitely better than they had the last time he had seen them, were folded and neatly piled just outside Marcia's door. He managed to get into them without help or indeed any great amount of discomfort.

"Next time I see him," Raider said, "I'll get Doc to pay you for this." He smiled. "I'd do it myself, but..."

"Yeah, I know." She shrugged.

Raider headed for the door, then stopped. "I just had a lousy thought."

"Yeah?"

"I'm broke, and I can't draw any more expense money without people wondering where it came from. Just in case there was some connection between that robbery last night and the reason I'm here."

"So?"

"So I'm supposed to hire you again tomorrow night."

"I can take care of that."

"How?"

She grinned. "I'll talk it around about what a fine, lovin' fella you are. Sweet. You know?"

Raider laughed. He couldn't help it. "Sweet" was not the way he would normally expect to be described.

Marcia's grin got wider. "Anybody that's interested will

just think I'm stuck on you an' givin' it away. It ain't like I haven't done that sorta thing before."

"It looks like I really do owe you." Raider let himself out and went downstairs. The trip was much more comfortable than it had been going up the stairs that last time.

The clock over the mirror behind the bar showed 11:35, and the saloon was nearly full. Loud-talking men were grouped at the end of the bar where the free lunch had been laid out.

Raider was ravenous. He headed for the free lunch, then remembered barely in time that he was quite completely broke. He couldn't even afford the nickel it would take to buy a beer and a plate of the "free" lunch. His stomach rumbled in protest against that injustice.

He walked on out to the street and turned left, toward the Grand Paree. He looked in the alley where the one-sided fight had taken place during the night. He was acutely conscious of his hatless head and was uncomfortable without a Stetson to shade his dome. There was, of course, no hat still lying in the alley, and he grumbled the entire two blocks to the hotel where he was registered.

At least he had paid for a week in advance when he checked into the hotel. He had a place to stay anyway, and probably they would let him sign for his meals in the restaurant that was attached to the hotel. He damn sure hoped they would.

First he went up to his room, though, thinking that he might have tossed some stray coins into his bag. Too much small change in a man's pocket was annoying, and sometimes he did that without thinking about it.

Besides, he wanted the spare revolver he carried in that same bag. He felt naked without a gun, worse even than being without a hat.

The Grand Paree was the largest and finest in Leadville, three stories high and ornately furnished. He climbed the stairs, wishing he had had the forethought to request a room on a lower floor.

Aw, shit, he told himself when he reached his room. The

door was unlocked. He distinctly remembered locking it before he left the evening before.

The room had been emptied of everything he owned. It was not just that his bag had been rifled. The bag and everything it contained had been taken.

And the changes of clothing from the wardrobe. Everything.

"Shit!" he said out loud.

A maid passing in the hallway gave him a startled, disapproving glance and scuttled quickly away.

Raider glared after her, not even tempted to apologize. He went back downstairs, wondering just what the hell he should do now.

His freshly cleaned clothing and the gaudy stickpin in his tie still gave him the front he was supposed to have, but there was nothing to back it up. The damn stickpin was just so much cut glass, worth a few cents to anyone who knew what he was looking at.

"Shit," he said again as he crossed the lobby and went into the restaurant.

He stomped his way to a table toward the back of the place and ordered the biggest damn steak they could wrestle out through the door to the kitchen. He didn't bring up the question of whether he could sign for the meal. There would be time enough to worry about that later.

While he was waiting for the food to be brought, he looked around the dining room. It was filled up with the lunchtime crowd. In a place like this there were no patrons in grubby mining clothes. The people who dined here, many of them with their ladies, were respectable, if not necessarily wealthy.

While he was watching, Charles LeFarge entered the room. The tall, fine-looking Frenchie saw Raider about the same time Raider spotted him.

LeFarge smiled and made his way through the tables to Raider's.

"Mr. Jones," LeFarge said. Raider stood and shook the hand LeFarge offered.

LeFarge looked around the room. The place was filling, but there were still a number of tables vacant where he could have sat. "May I join you?"

"Please do," Raider replied, his tone of voice and his gestures aping that lazy, safe son of a bitch Weatherbee. At last his association with the cuss was paying off.

LeFarge pulled out a chair, and both men sat.

"Forgive me for being blunt, Mr. Jones, but have you suffered an accident?"

For a moment Raider did not know what LeFarge meant. Then he remembered that his face was probably bruised from the night before.

"Something like that," he said.

"Sorry to hear that."

The waiter came with a menu, and LeFarge made a long and fussy production of examining it. He consulted with the waiter several times before ordering stuffed partridge, glazed carrots, and mushrooms in a wine sauce. Then he ordered a bottle of something that Raider could neither pronounce nor understand.

Raider's opinion was that the mere thought of all that high-toned shit should be enough to give a man indigestion, but LeFarge seemed pleased with his selections. So did the waiter. Or at least the soft-looking little pipsqueak acted like he did.

Raider's meal was brought, and he picked up his knife and fork, ready to attack it.

"Don't wait for me," LeFarge said. "Enjoy your meal while it's hot."

Raider nodded. The thought of waiting had not occurred to him.

He was more than ready for the meal, and he was almost finished by the time LeFarge's order arrived. Raider belched into his napkin and polished off the last of the rolls he had been given. He felt better after a night's sleep and with a good meal under his belt.

The waiter apparently assumed they were together and brought Raider no bill. When LeFarge was done, the bill was delivered. LeFarge picked it up, examined it, and placed a ten-dollar gold piece on the table. "My pleasure," he said.

Raider thanked him.

"Tell me, Mr. Jones, would you, uh, have a few minutes to spare this afternoon?"

"I'm not really in the mood for cards, if that's what you have in mind."

"In fact it is not, sir."

"Then I reckon I could spare you some time." Raider's intention had been to give LeFarge plenty of time to recognize him over the card table, but now that would be impossible. This offer, so soon, came as an unexpected bonus.

"I have a suite of rooms upstairs," LeFarge said.

Raider nodded and let LeFarge lead the way to the second floor. He noticed that the entirely too successful master thief did not bother to ask for change from his eagle.

Even in a place like the Grand Paree, Raider was surprised by the suite LeFarge took him to. The entry passed through a small foyer—useless but very attractive and classy—into a plush and rather large sitting room. There were other doors leading off to both sides, presumably to bedrooms that would be part of the fancy suite.

Whatever else the man was, Raider thought, Charles LeFarge knew how to live well.

A harpsichord sat in one corner of the sitting room. There was no one playing it at the moment, but sheet music spread open on a stand above the keyboard indicated that the thing was functional as well as decorative.

LeFarge motioned Raider toward a fancy, French-looking chair near the windows and crossed the room to a sideboard.

"Drink?" he offered.

"I wouldn't mind."

LeFarge nodded and poured brandy for each of them. Brandy was not exactly Raider's taste, but it would do. He accepted the glass and smelled of it, then cupped the balloon-shaped snifter in his hand the way he had seen

Doc do and swirled the liquid about. There was supposed to be a reason for doing that, he knew, but he was not sure what it was.

LeFarge nodded approvingly. "You are really doing quite well."

"Pardon?"

LeFarge smiled. "I said you are doing quite well"—the smile got wider—"Mr. Raider."

A few feet behind Raider's head, somewhere in the direction of one of those doors leading into another room, there was the faint but ugly sound of a pistol being cocked.

LeFarge was still smiling.

Raider had time to think that he hadn't liked this damn plan of Allan's to begin with. He was not liking it any better now.

Piss on 'em, one and all. He toasted LeFarge with the brandy snifter and took a sip of the fiery stuff. No, he still did not like brandy, either.

# CHAPTER EIGHT

Still smiling, LeFarge set his brandy aside and came across the room to frisk Raider for weapons. He seemed surprised to find that he was carrying none.

Raider shrugged. "Happens that somebody got there before you. My money too, if that's what you're after. Though to tell you the truth, mister, I wouldn't have taken you for a plain old stickup artist." He still had no idea who was behind him, but the sound had been warning enough.

He reminded himself to be careful *not* to let LeFarge know that Raider was aware of who and what the man was. That was not part of the plan and could well be the kind of slip that was fatal. Raider took a sip of the brandy.

LeFarge resumed his chair. Sometime between when he had turned away from Raider and when he sat, a compact derringer with twin muzzles had appeared in his hand and was now loosely aimed across the room in Raider's general direction.

Footsteps sounded behind Raider, and the person with the gun came around him to take a seat on the small settee near LeFarge.

Raider gaped. He couldn't help it.

She was ... he searched for the right word. "Lovely" was the only thing he could come up with, but that overused word hardly did her justice.

Her hair was a pale blond so light it was almost without color. It was done up not in the usual mass of tight curls but in a smooth, complex twist.

She was tall and slender, her neck a fragile column that seemed to emphasize the delicacy of her throat and achingly lovely face.

She had a haughty, hollow-cheeked patrician look of sheer elegance.

Her eyes were large and wide, a very pale gray. They were calm and gentle despite the tiny, seven-shot Colt's patent .22 revolver she was now slipping into her handbag.

She looked like the kind of woman who should be surrounded by fawning, foppish young nabobs, all of whom would want only to declare their affections for her.

She looked untouchable, as if a vulgarity would send her into a dead faint.

Yet she was in the suite of a dangerous, even a deadly, thief. And she carried a gun in her bag.

Raider was unsure how he should take her. There were no introductions that might have let him better understand what a woman like this was doing in the company of Charles LeFarge.

"No protest of your identity, Mr. Raider?" LeFarge asked.

Raider shrugged. "When a man holds a gun on me I kinda figure it's best to keep my mouth shut till I find out what he wants," Raider said.

"Do you know me, Mr. Raider? Or 'Mr. Jones,' if you prefer?"

Raider shrugged. "Only by the name you gave me last night. Should I know you?"

LeFarge smiled. "No, but by happy coincidence I do

happen to know you. Admire you too, for that matter. It was a very nice touch, stealing the Pinkerton Agency's own payroll. I salute you, sir." He raised his glass toward Raider, then drank.

"I don't know what you're talking about, of course." Raider said.

LeFarge laughed. "Of course not. You, uh, do know, I suppose, that I could turn you over to the Pinkerton Agency and receice a reward of several thousand dollars."

"For a guy named Jason Jones? I wouldn't know about that."

LeFarge laughed again. "A cool customer, Mr. Raider. I like that about you too."

"Thanks, Charlie, an' I think you're a real swell fellow. So why are you holding that gun on me?"

"Sorry. I quite forgot." LeFarge tucked the little gun back into his sleeve. It took him a moment to fit it back into the spring-loaded mechanism he wore there. Very quick, Raider knew. Unless something happened to make the spring gun hang up. More than one man had died as the result of a temperamental gadget like that failing to function when it was most needed. Raider wouldn't depend on one of the things himself, but he wasn't willing to trust his life on this one's possible unreliability. Certainly it had worked well enough the first time LeFarge used it.

"Better?" LeFarge asked.

"Considerably," Raider said. It was the truth. Life was generally more relaxed and comfortable when there wasn't someone pointing a gun at you, he had found out over the years.

"Cigar," LeFarge smiled. He was still looking at Raider, but the word had not seemed like a question or an offer. For a moment Raider couldn't figure what the man meant. Then he did.

The woman, whose name Raider still did not know, rose lightly and elegantly from her position on the settee and crossed the room to a table under the windows. She took a cigar from a rosewood humidor there, clipped the end neatly with a silver set of nippers, and struck a match. It took her half a minute or longer to warm and light the cigar. Then she carried it to LeFarge. He accepted it without thanks, without even acknowledging her except to take the now burning cigar from her hands. She returned to her seat on the settee.

Interesting, Raider thought. He wondered just what her relationship was to this strange and deadly man. LeFarge, as Raider well knew from the research done on the man, had been responsible for a great many robberies and a great many resulting deaths. But he had planned so well, and held himself so far removed from the actual execution of his plans, that no one had ever been able to charge him with any of his crimes, much less convict him of them.

Smoke from LeFarge's cigar drifted across the room toward Raider. It didn't smell as noxious as the stink-sticks Doc favored, but the same sense of welling nausea gripped Raider's gut.

LeFarge must have seen the look of distaste on Raider's somewhat battered face. He smiled. "Very good," he said. "As usual my information has been correct. And forgive me, please, for causing you discomfort. A small test of identity, you see."

"No, I reckon I don't see."

LeFarge held the cigar out to the side. The woman rose again to take it and lay it aside in a silver ashtray where it soon went out.

LeFarge crossed his legs and leaned back comfortably in his chair. "A reassurance for my own satisfaction before we discuss business, Mr. Raider," he said.

"Business, Mr. LeFarge?"

"You are in a position to help me, Mr. Raider. And I am in a position to help you."

Raider's eyebrows went up.

"You mentioned a moment ago that you have been robbed. I presume, sir, that you are without funds."

Raider nodded.

"As you may have gathered, I am, uh, not without resources."

"So?"

LeFarge smiled. "I would be happy to assist you in your moment of financial embarrassment."

"In return for what?"

The smile returned. "I have reason to believe that you possess certain information that would, uh, be of interest to me."

"I do? Or this Mr. Raider does?"

LeFarge laughed. "Very good, sir. I approve of your caution."

Raider shrugged.

"As I understand it, Mr. Jones," LeFarge said, "you have knowledge of a certain, uh, shipment soon to leave Leadville en route to San Francisco." He paused. "No comment, sir?"

"Not right now." Raider took a sip of the brandy. It was warming; he had to give it that much.

"What I suggest is a . . . partnership of sorts. A pooling of information, as it were."

"Why should I want to go partners with you, Mr. Le-Farge? I don't know you. Don't know anything about you. So why should I want to share information with you?"

LeFarge's smile grew. "The endeavor that interests us both, Mr. Jones, is not something that can be undertaken by one individual. You know that quite as well as I. And believe me, I have researched the subject thoroughly enough to know that. So have you. What you have to offer this partnership would be your, shall we say, specialized knowledge. What I have to offer is the manpower and the expertise to carry out the final plans made on the basis of that knowledge."

"You're talking in circles," Raider said bluntly.

"I am being circumspect, sir."

"Bullshit."

The lady seated near LeFarge, who looked as though she should have fainted in reaction to the word, seemed not to have noticed it.

LeFarge sighed. "Very well, Mr. Jones. It seems that my information has been correct on that subject also. Your pretense to quality is but a veneer."

"Get to the point, asshole." This time the elegant woman-an's eyes cut toward Raider. But he thought they held in-terest rather than condemnation in the deep, gray depths of them.

"I want to know everything you know about the shipment of gold planned in the very near future, Mr. Raider."

"And if I tell you?"

"As I said. A partnership. Including a more than fair distribution of the returns. Your pockets will be well filled again."

"What if I don't wanta go into this partnership of yours, Charlie?"

LeFarge gave Raider a tight-lipped smile. "Then I shall have no choice but to shoot you and collect the reward being surreptitiously offered by your former employers."

"Persuasive son of a bitch, ain't you?"

"So I have been told, sir."

"I'll think about it."

Raider was taking a chance. The partnership with Le-Farge was exactly what he and Doc and the agency had been planning on ever since the railroads had come up with this idea to trap the entirely too successful LeFarge. But if Raider accepted the offer too quickly, too easily, that fact could be enough to make LeFarge smell a rat.

On the other hand, if Raider refused out of hand, he could find himself dead.

There was only one way to play it, though, and to do that he had to take a chance.

Raider stood and turned his back on the smiling, smug Mr. Charles LeFarge. Turned his back and headed for the door in long, sure strides.

Outwardly he showed confidence with every step he took.

But the truth was he was half expecting to hear a faint click from LeFarge's spring-loaded derringer rig and to feel the jolt of a .32-caliber slug.

A hand-span-size area in the small of his back tightened and tingled in anticipation of the bullet, but there was noth-ing in his appearance that would have shown anything but complete calm and confidence.

He reached the door and got the hell out of there. He was sweating by the time he reached the stairwell landing.

# CHAPTER NINE

Raider drifted along the streets of Leadville for a half hour. He would have enjoyed going into one of the many saloons for a little time-killing relaxation, but he had no money and could not let that be known. He was still supposed to be putting on a front as a well-heeled gentleman named Jones. The big fish had already nibbled at the bait, but there were plenty of smaller fish in Leadville who might have heard about the Pinkerton reward for a man named Raider. And that quiet want order was real enough. It had to be if they expected to fool LeFarge with it. So to everyone else in Leadville, Raider had to *be* Jason Jones.

Raider didn't really feel like walking. He was still aching and sore from the pounding he had taken during the night. But he wanted to show himself where Doc could spot him and know that Raider was still on the job. Know too that Raider had been beaten.

Raider almost smiled, wondering how by-the-book Weatherbee was going to report that bit of information. He knew good and well that that damned Doc would have to report it. The old-maidish son of a buck reported every damn thing. Even if it put him in a bad light, which this little bit of information might do. After all, Weatherbee was supposed to be Raider's backup man on this job. Without anyone knowing it.

Pinkerton and the damn railroad nabobs probably never thought how impossible a position that was. A man couldn't act as a backup and still make sure there was no connection between them. No way. But Pinkerton might not have considered that. The railroad rich boys almost certainly had not.

Raider chuckled to himself, thinking that this time Doc's insistence on filing all the idiotic reports the agency demanded might put the old fart in hot water with the home office.

Serve him right, Raider thought. After all, Raider was the one taking all the chances here. Weatherbee was just hanging around for an easy ride. It would serve him right if Allan Pinkerton got pissed off at him for something Weatherbee had no control over.

Raider couldn't see Doc, wherever the lazy bastard was lurking. Or supposed to be lurking, anyway. That was his job this time. To be there watching, making sure that nothing went too seriously wrong.

Huh. Fat lot of good Doc had been last night when those yahoos jumped him in the alley.

Raider wondered who they had been. And whether LeFarge had been a party to it. Probably, Raider decided. But not personally. That was the sort of dirty work that LeFarge would not consider doing for himself. LeFarge seemed the kind of bastard who would order things done but not want to dirty his hands by joining into it.

Not that Raider blamed him in a situation like this one. LeFarge wanted Raider to enter into a partnership with him. He wouldn't want to risk exposing himself to the very man whose help he needed.

But still Raider suspected that LeFarge had ordered the robbery. The fact that his room had been cleaned out too was the give-away there. LeFarge wanted to make damn sure he was too broke to hire his own gang and go after the gold shipment without the partnership.

Yeah, Raider thought, it made sense. And really it didn't matter if Raider was right or not. The fact was, he was now the bait he wanted to be, and Charles LeFarge was trying to swallow him whole.

Just the way they had planned it.

After a few minutes Raider made a game of trying to spot Weatherbee.

He walked up and down the hilly streets of Leadville, acting like a gentleman on an afternoon constitutional. He appeared to be paying attention to nothing in particular. In fact he was looking for that lazy damned Weatherbee.

Eventually he spotted Doc.

The grimy, shabby, mud-encrusted fat man seated in the litter of an alley beside one of the less reputable saloons of Leadville didn't look much like a first-class Pinkerton operative, but that was Doc all right.

Raider held back a snicker as he ambled on past. Doc dearly loved tailored clothes and elegant surroundings and beautiful women and a life of "quality." Or what his Boston-bred expectations said was quality.

So here he was dressed like a stinking rummy and sitting in the dirt while Raider sauntered past in a dandy suit made up just for the occasion and smelling of toilet water.

Shee-it, Raider thought. This right here almost made up for the nuisance of those pricks in the alley last night.

He walked past Doc without looking at him, nor did Weatherbee in his drunk's disguise appear to look at Raider. Or Mr. Jones, as he was locally known.

But the contact, such as it was, had been established. Each knew that the other was on the job and that things were proceeding more or less as planned.

Raider went back to the Grand Paree and climbed the stairs to his room.

He tried to unlock the door only to discover that once

again it was already unlocked for him.

Aw, hell, he thought. Not again.

He pushed the door open.

The handsome woman he had recently seen in Charles LeFarge's suite was seated patiently in the single chair in his hotel room. She looked as though she had been expecting him.

Raider automatically reached for his hat, forgetting for the moment that he was not wearing one. He went in and closed the door behind him.

He took his coat off, folded it, and laid it on top of the bureau, then reclined against the headboard of the broad bed with his booted ankles crossed. He looked like a man in complete control of himself and everything that was around him.

"I don't think I caught your name a while ago."

The woman—damn, but she was a high-toned looker—seemed just as much in control of herself. She inclined her head briefly in his direction and said, "I am Judith Moorehouse, Mr. Jones." Her voice was prettily accented. British, Raider thought, or certainly one of the Empire nations. She was not American by birth, he was sure of that.

Raider smiled at her. "Considerin' that you were pointing a gun at me a little while ago, Judy, I don't reckon I'll tell you that it's a pleasure meeting you."

She stiffened. "Miss Moorehouse, if you please, sir."

His answer was a twisted grin. Elegant appearance or not, Miss Moorehouse had shown already that she was a hired hand in LeFarge's outfit. She jumped when he said jump, and all her airs and snootiness were not going to change that.

He laughed and said, "Whatever you say, Judy."

"How dare you!" Dark anger flushed her handsome features, and she half rose from the chair.

"Bullshit," Raider said mildly.

"What?" She sounded disbeliving as well as furious now.

"You heard me, damnit. I said bullshit. What I meant was bullshit. You look real pretty, Judy. No question 'bout that. But you're Charlie's step-an'-fetchit. So don't come at me playin' the lady. I know better." He grinned at her. "Can I ask you something personal?"

She glared at him but said nothing.

"Does a classy broad like you sweat when she fucks, or do you stay cool an' icy then too?"

She came all the way out of the chair that time and lunged toward him, her arm swinging around in a slapping sweep that would have rattled Raider's brains if he had done the gentlemanly thing and allowed it to connect.

Instead he shifted upright on the bed and caught her wrist.

She swung the other, and he caught that too, laughing at her as he did so.

"Cretin," she accused.

Raider laughed again. "I ain't real sure what that means, Judy, but I'll bet I wouldn't like it if I did."

Squealing with frustrated fury, she tried to bite his arm. Raider turned her and wrestled her down onto the bed, partially covering her body with his own male hardness.

"You never answered my question," he said.

Her mouth worked like she was trying to spit at him, but nothing came out.

"You need to practice that," Raider said. "If you want, I can round up some o' the local kids. They'd prob'ly be willin' to teach you good spittin' techniques for a dime. Accuracy or distance, either one."

"You miserable, cretinous bastard," Miss Judith Moorehouse told him.

"Yes'm, you're probably right." Raider got up off her and lifted her away from the bed. He set her down on her feet and shoved her rudely back in the direction of the chair. "Now," he said, "why don't you tell me what Charlie sent you here to say."

Her mouth worked like she had a foul taste in it. Then she regained control of herself. She was breathing heavily, but otherwise she managed to look calm and refined again, except for a few strands of the white-blond hair that had pulled out of the French twist at the back of her head.

She sat.

Giving her a wry grin, Raider returned to his relaxed lounging on the bed.

"Monsieur LeFarge has requested that I invite you to dine with him this evening," she said with only a little tension evident in her voice.

"Is that it?" he asked.

"That is the extent of the message I was asked to deliver," she said. "My personal preference, however, would be for you to decline this offer and any other he may make to you." She smiled quite wickedly. "It would please me so to see you shot down in the street like the cur you obviously are."

Raider laughed. "Atta girl, Judy. Keep up your act."

She rose and gave him an icy glare, then turned and headed toward the door.

"Judy."

She paused.

"I'd still like to know if you sweat."

She stamped her right foot once and almost ran in her hurry to get out of his room and away from him.

# CHAPTER TEN

Doc shuffled his feet in the dust of the alley where he sat and shifted from one cheek to the other on the broken wood crate that was his perch for the moment. He was, quite frankly, bored. But he had to be able to keep an eye on the hotel where Raider had disappeared some time ago.

Damned, lucky Raider, he thought. Got the easy assignment this time. Able to live high on the hog while Doc was the one required to grovel around in the filth of Leadville's alleys and back streets like some mongrel cur.

Doc still wished he had been able to talk Allan Pinkerton into some more suitable—or comfortable—form of disguise. But Allan had had logic on his side. The frequent pairing of Weatherbee and Raider was simply too well known to the criminal elements. Anyone who had any degree of intelligence—which LeFarge certainly did, and in abundance—would immediately look for Weatherbee once Raider was spotted. And it was LeFarge's recognition of Raider that was the key to the entire plan. So Doc had to remain in deep cover on this assignment. It was the only way it could hope to work.

And work it should, Doc thought. Charles LeFarge was a bright man. Allan Pinkerton's plan was to prey upon LeFarge's abilities, turn his very strengths against him and use them to make the railroads safe from this organized man who was fast becoming a threat to every railroad in the West.

Doc reached into a pocket of the cavernous, sagging coat that covered his artificially thickened frame. In his role as a drunk and a beggar he could not be seen carrying the fine Old Virginia cheroots he favored, but he had managed to solve that problem. Before he left Denver to reappear here in his disguise he had laid in a supply of the excellent tobacco and cut each cheroot into halves, then pre-burned the ragged tips.

Now when he wanted a smoke he could take from his pocket an already chewed and discarded-appearing short smoke. Anyone observing him would think he had scrounged cigar butts from the gutter. The impression would strengthen his role—and still let him smoke.

He pulled a match from another pocket and lit his stub with satisfaction after a moment of hesitation when he first without thinking held the flame of the match some six inches in front of his clamped teeth. He had to adjust the flame backward for half that distance to finally find the charred tip of the cheroot and light it. It was a habit pattern he had never consciously noted but that remained with him now when his hand almost by instinct placed the flame where it normally should have been required.

A pair of respectable ladies strolled past the mouth of the alley where Weatherbee sat. One of them idly glanced in his direction. Even before she could quickly turn her head aside, the matronly woman's chin lifted in haughty disapproval and her nostrils pinched and fluttered. She sniffed loudly.

Doc restrained an impulse to come to his feet and doff his hat. Instead he shuffled his feet in the dirt and lowered his eyes, accepting the lady's disapproval as one of the prices he had to pay here in exchange for anonymity. After a moment, when the ladies were well on their way down the sidewalk toward whatever their destination might be, Doc rose creakily to his feet and, half bent over, shuffled off to another saloon-side watching place.

He spent the remainder of the afternoon like that, silently and patiently watching and waiting.

Once a cheerful drunk reeled out of the nearby saloon— Leadville had dozens of them, any and all of them operating at full steam at any time of day or night—with a bottle in his hands.

The man staggered and fell, bumping into Doc's ankles as he sprawled on the ground.

Quick fear flew into the man's eyes when he realized he might have given offense, for an unintended offense here might well be answered with a knife or a bullet.

Then the man calmed, seeing the grimy, disreputable appearance of the man he had jostled.

He got awkwardly to his knees and accepted Doc's help in gaining his feet. He laughed, probably in relief, and pulled a dime from his pocket.

"Here, pally," he slurred. "Getcherself a drink on me." He giggled for no apparent reason and lurched away.

Doc mumbled effusive thanks in the man's wobbly wake, then stood and made his way hesitantly inside the saloon to order the two beers that he would be expected to buy once he had money in his fist.

He tossed off the beers quickly, grateful for them in truth after the thirsty afternoon he had just spent, and helped himself freely to the cold meats and cheeses and pickled eggs that were spread out at the end of the bar. He was glad for the food, too. It had been a long time since breakfast, with only a shriveled apple in his pocket for lunch, and he couldn't afford to be seen eating well here in Leadville.

When he returned to the street, dusk had begun to come on. Lamps were glowing inside the buildings.

Across the street Doc could see into the dining room of the Grande Paree. The lamps and chandeliers were bright. He struck a weaving course across the street, having to dodge once to avoid being run over by a dray loaded with barrels of beer being transported from the rail depot to one or more of Leadville's saloons. He remembered barely in time to avoid displaying an unseemly agility in his movements and took a heavy fall in the dirt of the street, then limped on to the side of the excellent hotel.

He looked inside. That damned Raider, probably unappreciative of his creature comforts, was having dinner with LeFarge. The open neck of a wine bottle packed in a towel-covered bucket of shaved ice stood beside their table on a brass wine stand.

Doc hid a grin in the growing darkness. As much as he himself might have enjoyed the occasion that was taking place indoors, Raider was probably suffering the torments of hell from the enforced charade of gentility. The man simply did not appreciate the delicate textures and bouquet of a fine wine. Probably was thinking of it in terms of rat urine. Doc chuckled to himself, enjoying the thought of Raider's discomfort.

There were, he thought, certain compensations about this assignment.

Raider would probably be secure at the dining table for an hour or more, Doc thought. Time enough and more for him to relieve the pressure on his bladder that the beers had caused. Doc turned and slowly shuffled his way back through the alley that ran between the Grand Paree and yet another of the Leadville saloons. There was sure to be an outhouse back there somewhere, and he would need a certain amount of privacy in the privy if he expected to have time enough to get through the layers of cotton padding that so grossly enlarged his outward appearance.

He had to feel his way through the alley. There was little enough light in the streets now, and in the close quarters of the alley night had already fallen.

"Get away from me," a woman's voice snarled somewhere ahead of Doc. "Get away from me, you bastard, or I'll cut your balls off."

A man's deeper tones returned laughter to the threat, and a moment later there was the sound of flesh striking flesh. A grunt of effort and a subdued cry of pain.

Doc abandoned his slow, beggar's gait for a moment and hurried ahead to the end of the alley.

The light was too poor for him to see much, but there was enough to disclose a dark-haired woman in the short costume of a bar girl facing a much taller man in rough working clothes. The girl held a knife loosely in one hand. Her other hand was pressed against her mouth where a trickle of blood flowed.

She stabbed awkwardly toward the man's stomach. He laughed again and brushed the knife away with casual ease. The blade flew out of the girl's hand, and he stepped forward and took hold of the bodice of her skimpy dress and yanked it downward.

The seams tore, and the upper part of her clothing fluttered to her waist, exposing pale, blue-veined breasts. The man looked at them and laughed again.

"You done picked the wrong ol' boy to get choosy with, Lily," he said.

"If you're too cheap to pay me, Howard, you can go get yourself a crib girl. You smell like a damned buffalo skinner, and I won't go with you for less'n five dollars."

Howard laughed again. "You'll go with me, Lily, an' it won't cost me nuttin." Howard's hand flashed out without warning. He grabbed her left breast in a powerful grip and used that purchase to haul her toward him.

Lily's knee shot upward toward Howard's crotch, but he was expecting the attack. He caught her knee on his thigh and turned it aside.

The girl's fingernails raked toward his face, but he caught her wrist with his free hand, then let go of her breast and caught the other wrist. He transferred both wrists into one large hand and pushed, shoving her to her knees in front of him.

Her hand lashed back and forth in fury as he began to undo the buttons at his fly.

"Don't you ever wash, you son of a bitch?"

Virtue was hardly at stake here, but, damn it, there was such a thing as a woman's right of refusal.

Doc sighed and looked about him on the ground for a two-by-four or some other suitable implement. The only thing he could find was an empty whiskey bottle. He took it by the neck and moved up behind the distracted Howard.

With a touch of regret, Doc took careful aim at the back of the man's skull and whacked him with the bottle. The bottle was a good one. It didn't even break.

Howard's knees sagged, and he crumpled to the ground.

Lily looked surprised. She saw Howard lying unconscious on the ground and the unlikely benefactor who stood behind him. It didn't take her long to adjust to the changed circumstances.

With a smile of quick pleasure she leaned over the fallen Howard and dipped a hand expertly into his pockets.

"Uh uh," Doc said.

"What?"

"You have the right to refuse him, uh, service. I do not believe that gives you the right to steal from him."

"What are you, some kind o' do-gooder?"

"Something like that."

With a sigh she came to her feet. She fiddled with the torn cloth at her waist, oblivious to the display of her naked torso, than gave up on the tattered remnants of cloth and draped what she could over her shoulders.

"Excuse me," she said. She turned and stepped into the nearby outhouse that she must have been on her way to visit when Howard accosted her.

Howard stirred once on the ground at Doc's feet, then settled lower and began to snore. Doc wondered if the man would even remember the incident when he wakened.

Lily came out of the outhouse and seemed surprised to find Doc still standing there.

"Oh," she said, comprehension dawning. She shrugged.

"I guess I do owe you for helping me with that prick." She nodded toward Howard.

Doc laughed.

Even if he were so unfastidious as to want this overused woman—which he was not—he would have had to show her the false padding under his clothes in order to take her. And he was not willing to do that either.

The girl finally seemed to realize that she was being refused. She shrugged and let the hem of her skirt fall. "I don't carry no money with me, dearie, so if you wanta be paid, you got to settle for this."

"Perfectly all right," Doc said.

She sighed, apparently feeling that she owed him in spite of the refused offer. "All right, damn it. I'll French you. But just long enough to get it up, hear." Her nose wrinkled. "I don't like French much. I musta told that to Howard there a hundred times or more." She snorted. "Last time his li'l bitty ol' cock was washed was when his mama done the job for him, I'll bet. Bastard smells like rotten cheese, an' he always wants to shove it in somebody's mouth. Ugh." She shivered.

"Go back inside," Doc told her.

"You don't want nothin'?"

"Go back inside," he said again.

"You talk funny, you know that?"

He was beginning to regret his good deed. "Go back inside," he said. He shouldered past her and went into the privy that had been his reason for coming back here to begin with.

When he came out again Lily was gone and Howard was still snoring on the ground.

Howard's pockets, though, had been turned inside out. He had been picked clean, and no doubt Miss Lily was now somewhat richer than she had been.

Doc gave a moment's exasperated thought to human nature before he bent into his old man's crouch and shuffled back out to where he could watch the main street in case Raider might need him.

# CHAPTER ELEVEN

LeFarge once again poured brandy for both of them. They were back in the man's suite. Raider was full. He had to admit there had been more than enough food and drink already. But he hadn't really enjoyed the meal. Too damn fancy for his tastes, although that damned Weatherbee probably would have enjoyed it. Raider would have been much more satisfied with beef and potatoes than with the trout and vegetables LeFarge had ordered. That sort of puny crap just couldn't satisfy a man, as far as Raider was concerned.

There still was no sign sign of Judith Moorehouse. There hadn't been all evening.

Nor had there been any business conversation over the dinner table. LeFarge had acted all through the meal as though they were a pair of gentleman friends. The talk, what little there had been of it, had been about foods and wines, plays and opera. LeFarge had done most of the talking. Raider kept his mouth shut. He cared even less than he knew about the subjects that seemed to interest Charles LeFarge.

Now, though, they would be getting down to it.

"I assume you have considered my offer," LeFarge said over the rim of his brandy snifter.

"Uh huh," Raider said. It was time to drop his act with LeFarge. The public part of it anyway. He grinned and asked, "How'd you spot me?"

LeFarge set his glass aside and spread his hands. "All manner of information becomes useful in time. I do attempt to pay attention to my adversaries."

"Adversaries." Raider mouthed the word slowly, as if tasting of it. "I like that." He grinned again. "I thought I was doin' pretty good till you come along."

"Well enough to fool most, I daresay." LeFarge looked smug and satisfied with himself.

"Yeah, well, the cat's outta the bag now, I reckon."

"You haven't yet responded to my question," LeFarge said. "Nor to my offer."

Raider hesitated, staring down into the amber liquor in his glass. The timing was delicate here. Too quick an acceptance and LeFarge might become suspicious. Too long a rejection and the man might try to eliminate what he thought was his competition.

"You haven't really told me what you have in mind," Raider said.

"I believe you know what I have in mind," LeFarge said.

"Maybe. Or maybe not. After all, I'm just an innocent feller on a lark."

LeFarge threw back his head and laughed long and loud. "Such caution, Mr. Raider. Really."

"Yeah, well, I really would ruther you not call me that, Sharles. No tellin' what kind o' ears might be around."

"We have complete privacy, I assure you."

"Yeah?" Raider stood. Quietly he crossed the room to the bedroom door where Judith had been hiding earlier in the day. He pulled it open to find her standing there, obviously listening to everything that was being said in the sitting room. She glared at him.

"Private, huh?"

"Miss Moorehouse is familiar with my, uh, activities. She constitutes no threat to either of us."

"Bullshit," Raider said.

LeFarge motioned for the woman to join them. She did, holding her skirts aside as she swept past Raider, as if trying to make sure he didn't contaminate her with the slightest brush of his clothing against hers. Raider noticed the gesture and laughed, which seemed to make her all the angrier.

"Another partner?" he asked as he returned to his chair.

"Not exactly." LeFarge beckoned to her and pulled her into his lap. He crudely cupped one of her breasts in his free hand.

"I see," Raider said. LeFarge's action was a declaration of ownership as much as a cattleman's brand being burned onto the hides of his livestock.

Judith acted as though she was unaware of the touch.

Raider grinned at her, and she colored. She turned her head away and tried to ignore the lean, handsome, mocking man in the other chair. Delicately, as if she were reaching for a pastry at teatime, she removed the snifter from LeFarge's hand and took a small sip. She returned the glass to him and sat with her eyes downcast.

"Now, Mr. Raider. What do you say?"

Raider pretended to think it over. "We might could work together," he said.

LeFarge smiled. "I hoped you would prove to be a sensible man."

"There's some things I'll need, though. Bein' broke and all that."

"Such as?"

"Hotel room an' meals an' some spendin' money."

"Of course." LeFarge nodded.

"And half the take when we get the job done."

"Impossible."

"You said you wanted a partnership. T' me that means fifty-fifty, bub."

"Impossible," LeFarge repeated. "I have a larger organization than you might realize."

Raider shrugged. "All of nothin' is still nothin'. You need what I already know, Charlie."

"Your information would be helpful," LeFarge said. "It is not necessary. I can accomplish the task without benefit of your services."

Raider grinned at him. "Bullshit. If you believed that, Charlie, I wouldn't be sittin' here now. I'd be dead in an alley someplace."

LeFarge frowned. The expression was hardly more than a scant flicker across his patrician features. Then again his face was calm and controlled. "As I said—"

"Yeah, yeah, I already know. Fact is, Charlie, you and me can do better together than we could apart. I thought about that all afternoon. I kinda hate to admit it, but it makes sense. With your outfit an' my knowledge, we can take the shipment easy. Either one of us alone, well, maybe we could an' maybe we couldn't. It ain't a sure thing unless we're working together."

LeFarge smiled. "Precisely. But I couldn't possibly make a fifty-fifty split with you."

"What then?"

"Twenty percent."

"What do you keep?"

"Twenty-five. The remainder will be divided among my people."

"Uh." Raider steepled his fingers and peered at his hands in deep thought. "Twenty-five apiece." he said.

LeFarge shook his head. "That would deprive my men. I never do that."

Raider grinned. "All right, then. Twenty for each of us. Make the boys extra happy this time."

LeFarge grinned back at him. "I rather like you, Raider."

"Twenty apiece, then?"

"No. I only said that I like you, your style."

"You want the lion's share."

"I contribute the lion's share, sir. My organization is superb. No one could ever hope to match it." He let go of Judith's breast and shooed her to the settee.

Raider's eyes followed her.

LeFarge noticed his interest and smiled. "Twenty percent," he said, "plus a bonus."

"What's the bonus?"

LeFarge pointed a perfectly manicured finger toward Judith Moorehouse.

Raider laughed.

"Discipline," LeFarge said. "It is as necessary as fairness. Judith has been lacking in discipline of late."

Raider was still laughing.

"Do we have a deal, sir?"

Raider nodded. "Reckon we do, Charlie."

"One thing, Mr. Raider."

"Yeah?"

"Never refer to me by that absurd nickname again." LeFarge's eyes had become cold. He was deadly serious now. Raider sobered. LeFarge's manners had almost lulled him into forgetting what a thoroughgoing bastard the man could be.

"I'll try an' remember that."

"Do, please."

LeFarge stood and offered his hand to seal the deal.

"Good enough," Raider said and shook with him.

LeFarge turned and motioned curtly for Judith Moorehouse.

Slowly, with no pleasure at all, she came forward to stand with her head down beside her new master.

"Use her however you wish," LeFarge said. "I ask only that you return her in reasonable condition."

Raider could see that the woman's outward calm was a deception. She was trembling slightly.

He wondered what in hell he was going to do with a female who was now virtually his slave.

The worst part of it was that anything he might do that

would seem out of character in the slightest was sure to be instantly reported to LeFarge.

A gift? Hell, the man had simply covered himself by putting a spy into the bed of his "partner." Raider was not fooling himself about that one. He would have to remember not to forget it for a moment in the days to come.

# CHAPTER TWELVE

Raider locked the door behind them. Judith crossed the room silently, head bowed and shoulders slumped. She looked like a woman who had resigned herself to a fate worse than death. He was not sure, since she was keeping her face averted, but he thought she might have been weeping quietly.

"Look," he said, "this wasn't my idea."

There was no answer from her. She sat on the edge of the bed and began unbuttoning her shoes.

"Damn it, woman," he snapped, "I'm in this for the money. When I want a woman I'll go find me one that *wants* to share my bed. All right?"

She gave him a look of loathing. He had been wrong about one thing. She was not crying. Not this one. Her expression was hard and cold.

In a way, that made him feel better.

"Do you have any money in that handbag?" he asked.

Still she did not speak, so he crossed the room and took the handbag off the side of the bed where she had placed it. He opened it and rummaged through it.

The tiny Colt revolver—a lady's muff gun with a seven-shot cylinder and spur trigger—he appropriated and slipped into his pocket. The bag also held an assortment of combs and brushes and handkerchiefs and feminine doodads and a small purse containing twenty-three dollars in coin. He put the money in his own pockets too.

"That's a big haul, isn't it?" she said sarcastically.

"I don't know about you, but personally I'm hungry again," Raider said. "I want a sandwich or something. Are you coming or staying here?"

She gave him a look that was contemptuous and disbelieving at the same time. "Don't you intend to ravish me?"

Raider looked at her and laughed. "Ravish? What the hell kind of talk is that?"

"Surely you colonials have learned the language by now," she said. "Or perhaps not."

"Lady, you slay me."

"Cheerfully," she agreed.

Raider shook his head. "Are you coming or not?"

"Not," she said firmly.

"All right then."

He went downstairs and out onto the street. He had had enough of the Grand Paree's fancy crap for the time being. He found a greasy-spoon café where for a quarter he could get a thick sandwich of boiled beef and fresh baked bread and pie and coffee. He took his time about going back to the hotel and felt much better when he returned to the room.

Judith was still in his room, as he expected her to be. She was in the bed, the covers drawn up to her chin.

Her shoes had been positioned, neatly side by side, at the foot of the bed, but there was no sign of the rest of her clothing.

Raider smiled to himself. She was teasing him, wanting

to get him all worked up thinking she was there for the taking. Then she would be able to spurn him. Yeah, he was sure that was what she wanted. Hell, she was fully dressed under those covers. He was sure about that. He was not so sure about what LeFarge would do when he discovered that Judith was not following directions. But he was sure that whatever that was, she was willing to risk it.

Well, he was not going to be taken in by her, damn it. He reached down and took a grip on the sheet and snatched it away from her.

Son of a bitch!

Wherever her clothes were, in the wardrobe or folded away in a bureau, she was certainly not wearing them.

Her body was as elegant as the rest of her. Long and slender and perfectly proportioned.

Her breasts were firm, rounded mounds tipped with delicate pink, and her waist narrowed to an impossibly small dimension. Her legs were long and tapered under a full, mouth-watering swell of hip.

And damned if her hair color was not really and truly her own. The hair at her crotch was so pale as to be almost invisible.

Judith gave him a stare of disgust and contempt, then parted her legs and spread them wide to accommodate him. Her gaping sex was as pink as her nipples.

And as dry.

She turned her head away from him without a word and looked toward the wall.

Raider could see the slim, elegant lines of her throat, the rosebud shape of her ear, and the curve of her jaw and cheek.

She was beautiful. Lovely. The word came to him again. It seemed the only one that was really appropriate to describe her.

She hated him. That was obvious. She gave herself to him, but unwillingly.

"Shit," Raider muttered. He threw the sheet back over her and stomped to the other side of the room.

But there was nowhere else to go. Nowhere to send her, either. He had seen the look in Charles LeFarge's eyes when Judith was delivered to him, heard LeFarge's mention of discipline. He was beginning to get the idea that he would be doing this woman no favor by rejecting her and returning her to LeFarge. It was a dilemna Raider didn't want, but one that was his nonetheless.

It didn't help a whole hell of a lot that the sight of that wholly and beautifully female form had given him an erection that was painfully insistent in its demands.

"Shit," he said again.

He returned to the side of the bed and sat to kick his boots off. He shucked out of his coat, trousers, vest, and shirt but left his drawers on. He was tired, damn it. He was still aching and sore from the beating he had taken the night before. His stomach was full and now he wanted some rest. And he did *not* want to be burdened by Miss Judith Moorehouse.

He blew the bedside lamp out and stretched out on top of the covers. He could feel her beside him. She lay rigid and motionless.

Waiting for him to ravish her, he thought with a disgust that matched what she had been displaying.

What kind of man did she think he was anyway?

He closed his eyes and tried to go to sleep.

Raider woke to complete darkness with the sense that someone was quietly trying to shake him awake. His eyes opened to complete and sudden wakefulness.

Then he realized that no one was trying to shake him. It was only that the bed was shaking.

Disoriented by the strange bed and the dark, it took him a moment to remember that he had not been alone when he went to sleep. Judith was still beside him. It was her crying and trembling that had shaken him awake.

He thought about reaching over to touch and comfort her but realized that his touch would probably be less than welcome. He cleared his throat and asked, "Is there anything I can do?"

She began to sob harder then. Softly still, but now he could hear as well as feel her.

He thought she was going to refuse to answer him again, but after a pause of several minutes she said, "No." Her voice quavered and cracked in that single syllable.

"Do you want to go back to the suite?"

"No."

"What is it then?"

She wailed, a low sound of unreasoned misery, and began to cry all the harder.

This time he was unable to keep himself from reaching out to her. He slipped an arm under her shoulders and pulled her to him. She buried her face against his shoulder, her tears hot against his skin.

"Tell me about it," he suggested softly.

Talking about it seemed to be the release she needed. And probably, he quickly realized, the fact that the room was in darkness and she didn't have to see the person to whom she was speaking, that she could speak under a cloak of anonymity, would have helped make it more comfortable for her.

"I've been such a perfect fool," she said in her clipped, British accent. "Quite the fool, don't you know. Never satisfied, you see. Bored to tears." She sniffled.

"I could have stayed at home, done as was expected of me. Croquet on the lawns. Galas in the season. Riding to the hounds. Marriage to some pale, limp lad with better breeding than that of the horses in his stables. But I was such a fool I thought that not enough. A want of adventure, you see. And I have a cousin who came to your wild West in search of adventure. Hasn't been heard from in ages, but the gossip and speculation are rampant. He's alive, of course. Still draws his remittance twice annually, so the family know he survives. I came after him. Seeking adventure for myself, not Lanny."

Raider began to stroke and pet the back of her head. He was too, too conscious of the feel of her naked flesh beyond the thin sheet that separated them.

"I fell in with Charles and was mad enough to think him

dashing." She laughed, but there was no humor in it. "The dashing gentleman with his mysterious resources and great power. That is the way he presents himself to the world. Now I know better, you see.

"The man is no better than a beast. He charmed me first so that I gave myself to him willingly. It was part of the great adventure, you see. I wanted that, too. I'd never lain with a man before Charles. Even had I wanted to at home, none of the boys there would have taken me. They would have been too shocked by the idea to've performed. Not like Charles. He performed quite well. Then.

"It was only later that he showed himself to be the kind of man he is. He used me all he wished. Then, once, when I displeased him, he gave me to his mates.

"Crude, horrid types they are. Simply horrid. Yet he gave me to them and laughed when I objected." She hesitated. "I am not brave when it comes to physical pain, you understand. Charles knew that. He let his mates have me, and then he hurt me. Made me do all manner of vile things with his mates. It hurt something fearsome.

"He likes pain, though, he does. I've seen what he's done to some of the doxies he hires for that. Tears them up proper, he does. I think someday he may do as much to me, though so far he's preserved me from scars. He likes to cause me pain but seems not to want it to show afterward. With the poor whores he doesn't care about that, o' course. It doesn't matter a lick to him what a mess he makes of their poor bodies." The flow of words had replaced the flow of tears now, and she seemed somewhat calmer.

"You won't tell him I said any of this, will you?"

"No," Raider told her.

"Will you help me? Will you protect me from him?"

Raider had the unpleasant thought that this whole thing might well be a trick staged by LeFarge to test Raider's loyalty, however temporary, to their partnership.

"I won't do anything until after this job is done," he said. "That comes first. Then we'll see."

"I can be very good for you," she said. "Just don't hurt me, please. It's the pain I mind, you see. I am quite used to the rest." She shuddered.

If she was acting, Raider thought, she was doing a damned good job of it.

"But I can be quite good. Ever so many of Charles's friends have told me so."

Her arm snaked out from under the sheet and she reached for him.

Raider was not particularly pleased with himself for being erect while he was listening to her troubles, but he was. She touched him and nuzzled against his neck.

"I'll be quite good to you."

Raider wanted to tell her that she didn't have to do this. That she was not obligated to him.

He said nothing, the touch of her hand and the memory of that perfect body claiming him and heating his blood beyond his capacity to resist.

It wasn't like she was some shrinking virgin, he told himself.

Aloud he said nothing.

Judith slipped out from under the sheet. Her flesh against his was cool.

Her lips, encircling the head of his cock, were warm. She held him loosely inside her mouth, touching him only lightly with her lips so that every throbbing pulse sent the tip of his cock thudding against the roof of her mouth.

The contact, too light, was not enough to do more than tease.

He reached down to her and dragged her back into a supine position at his side. He felt her spread herself open to him, and he raised himself over her.

Judith stroked him and guided him to the tight, furry entrance he needed.

Raider thrust forward quickly, roughly. She was not yet wet and was extremely tight. He thrust deeper into her body and felt the heat of her close around him to grip and hold him.

Judith raised her hips to him so he could penetrate her fully.

Her arms and legs tightened around him as he rocked in and out, faster with each succeeding stroke.

His breath began to come heavy in his throat, and his

muscles bunched and tightened as a swift wave of impending climax rushed through him.

Judith's pelvis humped and bucked beneath him, urging him on, drawing him closer and closer to the brink.

She pulled the orgasm from him and arched herself to meet him as he lunged and stiffened with one final, powerful thrust and spewed superheated juices into her.

Slowly, a fraction of an inch at a time, she released her hold on him and let herself slide away from him until she was limp and relaxed on the bed under him.

Raider relaxed too and lay back beside her.

Judith nuzzled his neck and ran her tongue lightly down his chest and across his belly. She lifted his limp cock into her fingertips and with her tongue cleaned him of the juices he had just spent in her body.

Raider reached down to run his hand over the curve of her back and side.

Son of a bitch, he thought.

She really *didn't* sweat.

# CHAPTER THIRTEEN

Charles LeFarge pulled out a handsome watch in a gold hunt case and consulted it, then snapped the case shut and returned the watch—which was worth more than most men earned in a month's time—to his vest pocket. He shoved aside the pencil and notepad he had been using all morning to record notations.

"Lunchtime," he said. "Shall I have something brought up?"

Raider stood and stretched. He didn't bother to hide his yawn. "I'd rather go down an' eat, if it's all the same to you. Need to move around some anyhow after sittin' all morning."

"As you wish." LeFarge smiled thinly. "If you think we have enough time to spare."

Raider returned the smile. Exactly which of the four

91

shipment dates was to be used—three of which were blatant decoys intended to frustrate the plans of anyone like Le-Farge—was one piece of information he had kept to himself this morning.

LeFarge, in turn, had refused to tell Raider just how he intended to take the gold shipment once he had the information he needed.

Except for holding back the true shipment date, though, Raider had told the man the complete truth about the protection arrangements he himself had made before the railroad chiefs concocted their plan to trap LeFarge.

That had come about, Raider knew, because one of the railroad owners had received a tip about LeFarge from the Hodding Agency, one of the many would-be pretenders to the throne Allan Pinkerton had created for himself in the relatively new business of offering private detecting services.

Obviously the Hodding people had hoped to attract for themselves the job of stopping Charles LeFarge. Instead, the railroads had chosen to pay them for that specific piece of information but to trust the tried and true Pinkerton Agency with the protection of their gold.

And now Raider found himself in the position of telling the best train robber in the whole damn country about the plans Raider himself had made to guard the next Leadville shipment.

It was an awkward position to be in, Raider thought now. But then he could hardly complain about his work being dull or routine.

"Do you have any estimate of the amount to be shipped?" LeFarge asked.

Raider grinned at him. "O' course. Likely you do too."

"So I do. Should we compare notes?"

Raider shrugged. "I know mine's accurate. Why don't you scratch yours down on one of them infernal bits of paper you're always messin' with. I wouldn't mind a look at just how reliable your sources are, Charles." LeFarge did not seem to mind being called by his first name, but Raider had not pushed the man on the point of using a nickname.

"All right." LeFarge jotted down a series of numbers, folded the paper, and placed it on the table.

Raider nodded. "Fifty-five thousand that shoulda gone out last winter," he said. "Seventy-two from the spring shipment that couldn't roll. And another hundred twelve from the current gathering. All the mines but the Lacy Jane are shipping this time."

LeFarge smiled. He motioned toward the slip of paper, and Raider picked it up. It was there, all right. $239,000, written in pencil.

"Reckon you do hear a thing or two," Raider admitted. "Shall we go down to lunch?"

Raider was heartily tired of the fancy foods and thick sauces in the Grand Paree's dining room, but he made no objection when LeFarge led the way in there once again.

They were given a table near the front, where they could see and be seen. That, too, was LeFarge's choice. The man seemed to like to put on airs. Raider would have much preferred a quiet table toward the rear where he could see but where no one would be likely to notice him.

LeFarge's generosity with his tips brought them immediate and smiling service from the nearest waiter.

The waiter even spoke passable French, which sent both LeFarge and the waiter into fits of seeming ecstasy. Raider had no idea what his host ended up ordering.

"Steak for me," Raider said. "Cut thick and fried in a pan with plenty of grease. Taters on the side. And a beer."

Without a change of either voice or expression, the waiter conveyed his disapproval. But he did write down what Raider wanted.

Raider's beer and LeFarge's inevitable bottle of wine were brought at once.

"I don't see how you drink..." Raider began, his habit of criticism overcoming the many resolutions he had made to himself for the duration of this assignment.

He stopped short in mid-sentence when a short, heavy, balding man in a business suit entered the dining room. The newcomer, who looked like a salesman or possibly a wholesaler in town to line up new accounts, was greeted by the headwaiter and led to a table at the rear of the large room.

"Something is wrong, Mr. Jones?"

"Maybe so," Raider muttered. "You see that yahoo that just came in?"

"But of course."

"Know him?"

"I do not."

"Well, I do."

"From before, you mean?" He referred to when Raider traveled under his own name and worked for the Pinkertons.

"Uh huh, and this guy could be bad news, Charles."

"How is this, Mr. Jones?"

"His name is Donald MacDonald, and he's the one good thing this new Hodding Detective Agency has going for them. Used to be a Pinkerton operative. He worked back east then, but I met him a time or two. If he gets a good look at me, he's damned sure likely to recognize me even with this fuzz on my face."

LeFarge frowned. "Hodding I have heard of, but I do not know of your Mr. MacDonald."

"Give him half a chance an' you will. Pinkerton made the mistake of wasting him on simple shit. Thought a fat man couldn't get around fast enough or think fast enough or something, but that ol' boy over there ain't half as fat as he looks. Built like a rock but all squatty and chunky. Anyway, that's why he jumped over to Hodding when they opened up. They promised to give him jobs a man could set his teeth into. If I was you, Charles, I'd make sure to stay outta his way."

LeFarge turned his head to get a better, longer look at MacDonald.

"Is he lookin' this way?"

"No."

"Good."

"Perhaps I should have one of my people insure that the gentleman will not interfere."

Raider had too good an idea of what LeFarge meant by that. And while like any other Pinkerton operative he had no great love for the competition, he did not want to see another agency's people burned either.

"You do what you want, Charles," he said in a low voice, "but my advice would be to stay clear of him an' leave him be unless it comes right down to us or him."

"Why is this, Mr. Jones?" LeFarge's voice sounded as much threatening now as it did interested. Or more so. Raider knew his response had better have the right ring to it or LeFarge's suspicions would be flying high.

"Plain old self-preservation," Raider said easily. "We don't know what brought MacDonald here. Prob'ly something that has nothing to do with us. But if he turns up dead, there's gonna be a lot more than the local badges wondering why. Hodding would have half a dozen operatives in here inside o' twenty-four hours. And once the word got out, Pinkerton would send in a dozen o' his, too. Allan don't like Hodding worth a damn, but if somebody burns one o' Hodding's people it'd be like somebody whupping a cousin you don't like. You might not be able to stand the son of a bitch, but you can't let strangers beat up on family neither, so you up an' pull together till the need is over. You see what I'm trying to tell you?"

LeFarge rubbed the side of his nose and seemed to think it over. Then he nodded. "For the time being, perhaps. We will take no chances."

"That's exactly why I think we ought to leave MacDonald be. You might as well kick a hornet's nest as kill an operative. Me, I don't want to take that chance. We're too close to risk it."

"How close are we, Mr. Jones?" LeFarge asked.

Raider grinned at him but would not answer. He drained the last of his beer and tossed his napkin onto the table. "I'm gettin' kinda nervous with that man in the same room," he said. "Think I'll go have lunch someplace else."

"Yes, it would not do for you to be recognized now."

Raider waited until MacDonald was engaged with the waiter, then slipped out of the dining room and down the street.

He was hoping fervently that MacDonald's presence in Leadville had nothing to do with Charles LeFarge or with the impending gold shipment. He hoped the man was here chasing a runaway wife or some similiar bread-and-butter job that the Pinkerton Agency would not take on and that therefore was the lifeblood of the smaller, competing agencies.

Because, aside from the nuisance value of having another agency blunder into the middle of this job, there was also the very real and very worrisome problem of the want that had been placed on Raider's head for the duration of this assignment.

It had been impossible for the Pinkerton Agency to bait their trap without putting out an all-too-real pickup order for Raider. And an arrest now could queer the whole operation.

So it was for selfish reasons as well as concern about MacDonald's safety that Raider hoped the former Pinkerton would go somewhere else to conduct his business.

# CHAPTER FOURTEEN

"Where *is* he, damn it." Weatherbee paced back and forth across the worn and none-too-clean flooring in Marcia's room.

He had been there for nearly an hour already, and Raider was late. Not that it was so unusual for Raider to change plans at the last moment and never think to tell anyone. But still Doc was worried.

When that miserable Arkansas plowboy finally did show up, Doc was going to have a word with him about this. Possibly several words, in fact. Possibly a whole string of words. Harsh ones.

Damn him.

Doc paced some more and lit up one of his half cheroots. The smoke was pleasing but, under the circumstances, not relaxing.

Damn the man.

Already the inconsiderate SOB had put Doc's cover in jeopardy. Not that Raider was likely to care, but Doc intended to tell him anyway.

At the appointed hour, Weatherbee had been on the roof of the building, leaning out over Marcia's window so he could watch for the shutters to be opened before he climbed down.

A warm, golden spill of lamplight coming through the unshuttered window appeared at ten minutes before the hour, and for a change Doc had found himself pleased with Raider. Not only was the man on time tonight, he was a little early.

So Doc had swung out over the edge of the roof and climbed carefully down onto the windowsill.

He was in the process of letting himself into Marcia's room when he realized that a few feet away, Marcia was engaged in busily humping her rounded ass under a dark-haired man's sweaty figure.

Doc had thought that all the better. He always delighted in any opportunity to interrupt Raider in mid-stroke.

He had been prepared to do exactly that again, thinking that the dumb plowboy had come early so he could have a few minutes to jump Marcia before he and Doc got down to business.

Doc was halfway through the window before he realized that the man engaged in screwing Marcia was not Raider.

There was a bald spot on top of the man's head.

Otherwise, from that angle and while engaged in that particular horizontal activity, Doc couldn't see enough to realize he was climbing in on the wrong damn man.

He had been about to walk in—sort of—on some unsuspecting customer who had come here for a different kind of rendezvous from the one Doc and Raider intended tonight.

It was only the customer's preoccupation with Marcia's bumps and grinds that kept him from realizing he was not alone with his hired companion.

Marcia, with a look of bored disinterest, had not been so unaware.

She saw Doc at her window and, without breaking rhythm as she humped and moaned with feigned delight, waved Weatherbee away.

Doc had to climb back out onto the windowsill and hang there out of sight. It had been uncomfortable, but at least it didn't take long.

He could hear clearly while the customer loudly signaled his satisfaction with a groan. Marcia matched the noise with a shriek and babbled to the poor son of a bitch how very good it had been for her too. Then she helped the fellow on with his clothes and hustled him out of the room.

Doc gave her credit for the performance. And for the fact that she had not taken any time trying to wheedle an extra tip out of the customer. Generous of her, he thought.

He had heard the door close and a bolt slide shut, then she came to the window and helped him inside.

"Sorry," she had said. "He thought it was hot in here. Wanted some fresh air."

Doc had crawled through the window with his arms aching from the strain of hanging outside her window so long.

He had also, he had to admit, started to ache in another fashion when he watched Marcia pull her kimono over her shoulders. It had been rather a long time since he had been with a woman, and it was beginning to look like this disguise was going to prevent him from doing anything about that in the near future either. He was not so far gone, though, that he was willing to take sloppy seconds from a two-dollar bar girl.

All that had been an hour ago now, though, and Doc was becoming really worried.

"Should I look downstairs again?" Marcia asked.

Doc nodded. Every few minutes for the past half hour the girl had been stepping out to the head of the stairs and looking to see if Raider might be waiting downstairs for her to appear there.

She didn't want to actually go down and spend any time in the crowd of drinkers and gamblers below, because it would look awkward and unnatural if she had to refuse a paying customer's offer of short-time employment.

She slipped out into the hallway, closing the door behind her. She returned a few minutes later and shook her head.

"Damn," Doc muttered. He began to pace again.

He also began to scratch himself through the thick padding of his disguise. Apparently the quarters and the company he had been keeping lately had given him a supply of unwelcome livestock under the padding. At best it was going to hurt his pride to have to have himself deloused when this assignment was over.

Doc checked his watch for probably the fortieth time in as many minutes.

"I'm going to go out and check the inconsiderate idiot's room," he said. "I found a rooftop where I can look into it. At least I think I can, if I can find a way up there. If he show's up here while I'm gone, Marcia, tell the sorry son to wait for me. I'll be back."

She nodded.

"Leave the window open so I can get back in." He smiled at her. "And this time no strangers, if you wouldn't mind."

She smiled back at him, obviously not at all bothered to have had him watching while she hauled some stranger's ashes.

Doc made sure his padding and filthy clothes were all in order, then climbed back out into the night and up onto the roof. He was becoming almost accustomed to it by now.

He crossed the roof, checked to make sure there was no one in the alley below this time, and climbed back down to ground level. The only dangerous part of it would have been if he was discovered clinging to the side of the wall where no bum had any reasonable right to be—the logical conclusion would have been that he was trying to break into a room and steal something. Once his feet were on the ground he felt better.

Rather than walking the streets in public view, he hurried through the back alleys until he was opposite the Grand Paree, then limped openly across the public street and into the protective darkness of the alleys on that side of the block.

Observation from ground level had already showed him

where Raider's room was. He was past the Grand Parce, though, and entered an alley behind it.

He stopped beside a tall board fence and looked carefully around to make sure he was not being observed, then climbed quickly and easily over the fence and dropped to the ground again on the other side.

He had to pick his way through the litter of a weedy backyard at the rear of a boarding house. He could hear voices coming from inside the house and the shrill whistle of a teakettle announcing itself at a boil.

Doc reached the back porch of the house. There was a lamp burning in the kitchen at the rear of the house. He ducked back into the shadows when a hard-faced, middle-aged woman responded to the whistle of the kettle and hurried into the kitchen.

He could see her clearly through the window in the back door while she poured water from the kettle into a ceramic pot and covered the pot with a cozy. She put the pot on a tray that already held three cups and carried the tray back toward the front of the house.

Doc gave her a moment to make sure she hadn't forgotten anything in the kitchen, then reached for the roof support post over the back porch and shinnied up it.

He climbed onto the porch roof and stood on tiptoes so he could look across the alley into the lighted windows of Raider's hotel room.

What he saw made him curse under his breath.

No damn wonder the sorry son was late.

He had a woman in there.

And what a woman she was!

Tall and lithe, her hair an extraordinarily pale blond that was carefully groomed and coiffed.

She also happened to be naked. Trust that damned Raider for that, Doc thought.

She had a body that would have been a perfect model for a master sculptor, and she moved with languid grace.

Doc could feel an insistent pulsing in his crotch and had the unhappy feeling that he would not sleep well tonight.

He suspected that his dreams were going to be dominated by the memory of a slender female body of purest alabaster.

It was all going to be Raider's fault too, Doc thought with no particular satisfaction.

At the moment, however, Doc couldn't see Raider.

The woman was at the door that led out into the hotel hall. She slid the bolt closed and went to stand in front of the mirror. She took up a brush and began pulling it through a long fall of pale hair that spilled down over her shoulders and breasts when she removed the pins that had been holding it.

The upraised arms of the brush strokes did maddeningly interesting things to her breasts, which were firm and pink-tipped.

Doc groaned under his breath and inched higher on the sloping porch roof behind the boarding house. He could see the blond woman better than he really wanted to, but he could see no sign of that damned Raider.

He managed to get a little higher, with his back pressed against the peeling paint of the house wall, and again raised himself onto tiptoes.

He was able to get a glimpse of the bed now.

It was rumpled, the sheets discarded at the foot of the bed.

It was also empty.

Raider was not there at the moment.

Doc thought about it. The woman, whoever she was, had just been closing and locking the door when he first saw her.

And this was Raider's room. He was sure of that.

So, obviously, Raider had been delayed here by a romp with the blond woman.

Doc took another look at her and in spite of himself could not blame Raider for being late. Not this time. Not with a woman like that in his bed.

Logically, then, Raider must just have left for the meeting in Marcia's room.

Time and effort wasted, Doc grumbled to himself. Ever

since he had teamed up with the damned Arkansawyer, that
had been the story of Weatherbee's life—time and effort
wasted.

Doc let himself down off the porch roof and eased back
over the fence into the alleys of Leadville.

He began making his way back toward Marcia's room
and the planned rendezvous.

# CHAPTER FIFTEEN

Raider pushed his plate away, and Judith Moorehouse immediately and obediently took it and put it with the other litter from their meal onto the serving cart that had been brought up to the room. She was silent, as she had been ever since he returned to the room this evening.

The afternoon had been spent with LeFarge, going over the details of the gold shipment's protection plan until no slightest point had escaped the man's note taking.

Nothing, that is, except the shipment date. That Raider refused to discuss.

"I need a bare minimum of four hours advance knowledge," LeFarge had argued when he finally accepted the fact that Raider was not going to tell him the shipment time until the last minute.

Raider was impressed. All the more so because if Le-

Farge admitted to needing no more than four hours to mount his attack on the train carrying the gold, he really needed no more than two and possibly no more than a single hour to put his men into motion.

A response that fast would require a group of men who damn well knew what they were doing and who could be counted on to be ready when the time came. Raider was genuinely impressed by the efficiency LeFarge commanded from his men.

No wonder the man had become such a threat to the railroads, and no wonder his few but spectacular past thefts had been so stunningly successful.

LeFarge had seemingly come onto the scene out of nowhere. He was thought to have been involved last year in the theft of a currency shipment to a bank in Springfield, Missouri.

The job had been damned cleverly done, Raider admitted. There were no special guards employed in the mail car carrying the insured box of currency. But then no one was supposed to know that the money was being shipped, either. The mail coach guard himself did not know what his car was carrying.

The guard went on duty in St. Louis, ate his dinner from the pail his wife had packed for him, and fell promptly asleep. When he woke up the train was at the Springfield depot, and the box of currency was missing from the packages in the mail car. It was determined later that a sleeping potion generally available only to physicians and larcenous bartenders had been put in the water keg in the mail car.

No one had ever proven that Charles LeFarge was a party to that theft, but his name had been rumored in connection with it. Those rumors had been the first time anyone in the Pinkerton Agency had ever heard of Charles LeFarge.

A month later a similar incident occurred in the mail car of a Southern Pacific special operating between San Francisco and the Comstock region. A shipment of gemstones had been taken that time. The most discouraging part of it from the railroad's point of view was that the train had not been a scheduled run but was a special made up on train orders issued only hours before departure.

LeFarge was not exactly known to have been involved in that theft, but the method of operation pointed to him.

Railroads throughout the country immediately issued orders concerning the filling and use of water casks in guarded cars, but there had been no more known attempts to put mickeys in water containers.

Then this past winter an entire train had been stolen by a group of smiling, polite gunmen who had an accomplice stationed at a rail switch ahead of the freight special.

The train had been diverted from the main line of the Denton, El Paso & Pacific and shunted onto a spur line.

The smiling, genial robbers unloaded a military cargo of arms, ammunition, and payroll containers onto waiting bull carts, then coldly gunned down the unfrightened train crew to give themselves time to escape across the border into Mexico.

It was only Lady Luck that had given investigators any information about what had happened to the missing train. One of the train crewmen survived to tell about the robbery, although he would remain paralyzed from the waist down for the rest of his days. He had been shot through the back by a large, bearded man. The bullet had severed his spine but had failed to kill him.

Frantic—and expensive—inquiries made by a group of concerned railroads had come up only with rumors after that theft of an entire train.

Nothing had been learned about the missing payroll money, but the military cargo had been easy enough to trace. It surfaced again in the possession of a Mexican revolutionist general.

Informants in Ciudad de Acuna said the general had purchased the arms, for gold, from a gentleman who gave no name but who spoke French fluently. LeFarge was suspected, but again nothing could be proven against him.

The railroads, frankly, were becoming more and more concerned about LeFarge's presumed successes.

And now Raider was engaged in a partnership of sorts with him. At least as far as LeFarge was concerned. At least as far as Raider *hoped* LeFarge was concerned.

Now that LeFarge had most of Raider's useful information already written down in his notepad, there was a strong possibility that M. LeFarge might wish to dissolve the partnership.

The knowledge that the raid crew in Texas had covered themselves by way of cold-blooded murder did not make Raider feel any easier about his own vulnerability now. He damn sure hoped Doc was doing his job this time.

Doc Weatherbee. Thinking about Doc, Raider checked his watch for the time.

No problem. He had more than enough time to make his excuses and head over to the saloon where he was to meet Marcia and head up to the privacy of her room.

Raider's thoughts were interrupted by the sound of a sigh. He looked across the room to where Judith sat, chin high and hands folded in her lap.

She was as lovely as ever, but she looked sad.

"What were you thinking about?" he asked.

She looked startled for a moment. Then her eyes dropped away from his toward her lap. "You wouldn't want to know."

He smiled at her. "If I didn't want to know, I reckon I wouldn't have asked."

"Reckon," she mimicked, her mouth forming the word as if it were foreign to her. And probably it was. "Gentlemen do not use words like that, do they?"

Raider grinned at her. "Reckon they don't. But except for puttin' on an act, ma'am, I *reckon* I never claimed to be no gentleman."

Judith sighed again. "As a matter of fact, Mr. Raider, it is precisely that that had been occupying my thoughts."

Raider raised an eyebrow and waited for her to explain.

"I came to your continent to escape fops and dandies, but I found myself seeking out the company of gentlemen, you see."

"Reckon I don't see," Raider said.

"Charles is a gentleman. He is also cruel and abusive. I loathe him, but I lack the strength to escape him." She sighed. "You, on the other hand, are a simple rustic beneath your veneer." She hesitated, unsure if she might have gone too far and given the kind of offense that could have a painful return. When Raider did not react except to wait for her to continue, she smiled. "As I was saying, you are no gentleman, Mr. Raider. But you are a gentle man. Am I making any sense?"

"Oh, I think I'm followin' you all right."

"Good." She sighed again. "Everything I have been led to expect about breeding and the gentlemanly qualities is turned topsy-turvy in this strange world of yours. Yet both you and Charles are highwaymen at heart. It should be Charles who offers the excitement that I wanted. Yet it is you, sir, who provides it."

She looked at him, her eyes as wide as those of a startled fawn, when she realized the enormity of the admission she had just made.

Then, with a cry that might have been fear or might as easily have been longing, she lurched out of her chair and dropped to her knees at Raider's feet.

She wrapped her arms around his legs and pressed her cheek against him. She began to cry.

For a moment Raider didn't know what to do with this weird Englishwoman with manners and background that he couldn't even imagine.

But, hell, he realized, there isn't but one way to handle a crying female. He pulled her up into his lap and began to stroke and soothe her.

After a moment she relaxed against him and began to calm down.

The feel of her body against him, the scent of her hair took unwanted effect, and he could feel his desire for her becoming obvious.

She felt it too. She shifted on his lap, then gave him a look that was poles apart from the hatred she had displayed toward him the day before. It was embarrassingly close to adoration. He found that to be as unwanted as her hate had been.

Judith slipped off Raider's lap and down onto the floor at his feet. She quickly unfastened the buttons of her dress and shrugged it off her shoulders, exposing those superb breasts and—this time—hard-tipped nipples that were a declaration of her own desire.

The fact that this time she genuinely *wanted* him to take her was more surprising to Raider than anything else.

But the conclusion seemed inescapable. Any woman can fake passion. Any can pretend a climax. He knew of none, though, who could pretend to a visible arousal like that.

Judith removed her dress and stockings and tossed her underthings aside, then helped Raider out of his clothing too.

If he had been interested before, he felt close to the bursting point now. Her body was exquisite, and it was freely offered.

She took him by the hand and led him to the bed and pressed him down onto it. She smiled at him.

"This is something I've never really wanted to do until now," she said.

She bent over him and began laving his cock and his balls with her tongue. She took him deep into her mouth, warming and holding and manipulating him with her tongue.

Raider pulled her onto the bed beside him, careful not to dislodge her from what she was doing, and ran his fingertips through the pale fuzz that was her pubic hair.

This time she was wet, he noticed. Eager of her own volition to accept him there.

He dipped one finger into the heat of her body, then let it trail out again and through the moist valley of her sex.

He found the tiny button he wanted and gently fingered it.

Judith quivered and pulled her head abruptly away from him. "What . . . what are you doing?"

Raider smiled at her. Very lightly he rubbed her there.

"Ahhh." She sighed, a very different sound this time from the ones she had made earlier, and her eyelids drooped low with pleasure.

"I never...nothing like that...ever before. I didn't know..."

Raider smiled and continued with his titillation of her clitoris.

Judith's hips began to move slowly, in time with the soft motions of his finger. She pressed herself more firmly against his hand and closed her eyes. For the time being she was lost in the waves of sensation he was giving her, her former mission forgotten.

After a moment her mouth dropped open in surprise and her eyes opened wide.

She stiffened and shuddered, bucking softly under his touch and pressing herself hard against his knuckles.

She yelped out loud and went limp.

Raider was still grinning when she finally opened her eyes again and looked at him with gratitude and joy. "I never knew it could be like that for a lady," she said in her cultured British tones.

"Yeah," he said, "or even for a woman."

She sighed happily and remembered what she had been doing before she was so nicely interrupted. Once again she took him into her mouth, and this time she didn't stop until Raider pulled her away.

Even then she insisted on using her fingers to milk the last drops of liquid from him and plucking them away with the tip of her tongue.

"Nice," Raider admitted.

She gave him a smile that was oddly shy under the circumstances. "Truly?"

"Uh huh."

"I'm glad. I never have been before, you know. But this time I am quite truly glad that I pleased you."

They still lay side by side and head to crotch. Raider noticed that she even had a clean, fresh scent to her there.

Judith wiggled very slightly against the hand that still rested between her thighs. Shyly she asked, "Would you possibly consider...?"

Raider laughed. "Matter o' fact," he said, "I have an even better idea. An' if you think that first was nice, wait'll you feel this."

He pulled her closer. The first wet touch was enough to make her quiver and wriggle, and the second sent her into spasms of excitement.

It took only moments for him to send her shuddering and shaking over the brink.

And then it was her turn once again to give as well as she had gotten.

She brought him erect with her mouth again, but this time Raider pulled her unprotesting body into a new position and plunged deep inside her.

It was infinitely more satisfying for both this time than it had been the night before. This time she was wet, and as eager as he. Perhaps, he thought, she was more eager. She certainly acted like it.

And this time when he made that final, deep, satisfying thrust into the deepest recesses of her body, she joined him in a soft shriek of almost unbearable pleasure.

Raider felt proud of himself. It was a feeling he was not used to. At least not in connection with this particular type of activity. Yet he couldn't help feeling that he had shown her something she had needed to know for a long time.

He rolled away from her and looked.

He began to laugh.

"What is it?" she asked.

"Just a minute. Gotta check something." He lifted her arm and pressed his hand against the soft flesh there. And began to laugh harder.

"Ladies *do* sweat," he declared.

Judith grabbed a pillow and flung it at him.

"Oh, hell!" Raider sat bolt upright on the rumpled bed.

Judith looked like she was agonized by the thought that she might have done something to displease him. "What?"

"It's getting late," Raider said, "and I wanted to go out for a bit this evening." He had almost forgotten himself enough to tell her that he had to meet someone tonight. And no matter what she appeared to think of him now, he couldn't risk her reporting back to LeFarge on the things he did and everything he said.

He pretended calm disinterest while he went to the pile

Judith had made of his discarded clothing and checked his watch for the time.

He was already long overdue for the meeting with Doc, but he forced himself to take his time about dressing and giving Judith a lingering kiss goodbye.

"Lock the door behind me," he told her with a smile. "You're way too lovely for me to want to take any chances with, Lady Moorehouse."

For a moment she looked sad. Then she brightened and kissed him again.

She followed him to the door, even lovelier without her clothes than she was with them, and he waited outside in the hall for a moment until he heard the bolt slide closed. Then Raider hurried down the stairs and off toward his meeting with Weatherbee.

If the old bastard only knew, Raider thought with glee.

# CHAPTER SIXTEEN

Raider was preoccupied with thoughts about being late for the meeting with Doc. At least that was as much of an excuse as he had for not paying enough attention.

He left the Grand Paree and turned left, hurrying up the street toward Marcia's room over the saloon. He stepped off the board sidewalk in front of the hotel and almost immediately felt the all too familiar nudge of a revolver muzzle gouging him in the ribs. He came to a halt, thinking helplessly about the Remington revolver that no longer rode at his waist. The tiny .22 he had taken from Judith's handbag was doing him no good in the depths of his coat pocket; there simply was no way he could get it into action before any drunken slob would have had time to shoot him dead. With the Remington he might have taken the chance, but not with a pipsqueak .22 that might as well be under lock and key as where it was now. He sighed and turned to look at whoever was holding the gun on him.

"Evenin', Donald."

MacDonald, the Hodding operative, nodded to him pleasantly enough. "Good evening, Raider."

"I was kinda hopin' you hadn't recognized me this afternoon. I got to say you handled it well. Never noticed that you tumbled to me."

"Thank you." MacDonald smiled. He seemed genuinely pleased by the compliment.

"You, uh, could make me feel some easier if you put that gun away. Seein' as how we used to work together and all."

This time MacDonald shook his head. "Sorry, Raider. What I hear is that you've gone over to the other side. I don't think I should take the chance."

"Who, me?" Raider asked innocently. "Where'd you ever hear a thing like that?"

MacDonald chuckled. "You always were a cool one," he said. "I used to admire you quite a lot. Did you know that?"

Raider shrugged. Even that small hint of movement was enough to tighten MacDonald's grip on the blunt, ugly .455 Webley that was still digging into Raider's ribs. For a moment Raider was afraid the gun was going to discharge. "Nervous, Donald?"

"Damn right I am, Raider. I know you too well to trust you under these circumstances."

There were other people on the public street. MacDonald apparently didn't want to be disturbed by them. He jerked his head but carefully maintained his pressure with the muzzle of the Webley, gesturing Raider into the alley that ran between the Grand Paree and a nameless honky-tonk.

MacDonald looked nervous. Raider was experienced enough to know it's a fool's game to argue with a nervous man. That could become just another form of suicide. He eased along into the alley with the Hodding man.

He was also curious, though. MacDonald was taking him into the alley instead of heading immediately down the street toward the town marshal's office at the south end of Leadville or uphill toward the tall stone courthouse building where the county sheriff's office would presumably be.

"Something on your mind, Donald?"

The man nodded. "I want to hear your side of it, Raider. The truth, and all of it."

"What have you heard?"

"You know damn good and well what I've heard. The word is out on you, Raider. They say you jumped the fence and took a bundle of Pinkerton money with you. There've been no public announcements, of course. Allan would look like an ass if it got into the newspapers. But the word is out. Two thousand dollars for your return, Raider. And Hodding allows us to accept reward money."

"I'm surprised you're taking the time to talk about it," Raider said.

"It doesn't smell right to me, Raider. Doesn't sound like your style at all."

"Really?" Raider cleared his throat and gestured help-lessly with the hands that he had been carefully holding away from his sides. "Mind if I put these down? I'm getting tired."

MacDonald smiled. "I don't think it will kill you to keep them up where I can see them," he said. "But it might kill you to take them down."

"You sound serious."

"Good. I am."

"So what do you want from me, Donald?"

"Like I said, Raider. The truth. That holdup deal doesn't sound like you. Not when I knew you."

The temptation was certainly there. All Raider had to do was tell MacDonald the truth. That the whole robbery thing was a hoax intended to draw Charles LeFarge into a trap. That everthing was going according to plan. Except, of course, for MacDonald's interference.

That would be the easy thing to do.

But then MacDonald would know and so would anyone he told, whether he gave the information privately to friends or officially in a report to the Hodding Agency.

That was the problem. LeFarge's sources of information were still unknown and much too effective for Raider to want to take that chance.

Right now there were only a half-dozen men who knew about it, and that included Raider and Doc. Apart from them, there were only Allan Pinkerton himself and three railroad heads who knew the plan. Even the Pinkerton branch managers had been told that Raider was a thief and that Weatherbee was on leave of absence and presumably was trying to track down his former partner.

With the Pinkertons' own people kept in the dark, Raider did not want to let the Hodding Agency in on the scheme.

On the other hand, he didn't want to go to jail either. He wondered what would happen if MacDonald took him in. Would LeFarge manage to spring him somehow? Or would Charles simply make do with the information he had already obtained and leave Raider to his fate? Raider didn't really want to test it to find the answer to that question, but he didn't want to tell MacDonald the truth either.

He shrugged again and grinned. "You know how it is, Donald. Comes a time when the pickings are too big an' too easy. I reckon my time arrived. But I sure wish you hadn't recognized me today. I surely do."

"It's true, then? You really did take a Pinkerton payroll?"

"Ayuh, reckon I did."

"Well, I'll be damned."

"Me too, but I hadn't expected it quite so soon," Raider said.

"You're worth two thousand dollars to me in reward money," MacDonald said. "You know that, I suppose."

"I heard tell," Raider agreed.

"Well?"

"Well, what?"

"Customarily," MacDonald said, "this is where the felon tries to bribe an operative with the offer of a reward larger than that posted by, in this case, the Pinkerton Agency."

"Yeah, I'm kinda used to that too, Donald, but the only thing that ever done for me was to make me mad. You want

I should be dumb enough to make you mad, and you standing there with a big-assed revolver in my ribs?"

MacDonald began to laugh. "Your protests of purity come a little late, don't you think? After you've just admitted to robbery and all?"

"Yeah, I see what you mean."

"You really didn't ever take that kind of bribe, did you, Raider?"

He sighed. "Nope. Sounds foolish as hell now, I reckon, but I never did."

"I always used to admire you about that, Raider. I truly did. It was commmon knowledge that you couldn't be bought once you had a man, and I truly admired that trait. Thought you were an ass, of course, but I admired your honesty. Now we all discover that you're as venal and frail as the rest of us."

Raider's eyebrows went up a notch and then another. It was finally beginning to dawn on him where all this palaver was leading.

"Donald, do you mean to tell me that you might be willin' to let me walk away from here free an' clear?"

"Did I say any such thing as that?"

"No, but..."

MacDonald smiled at him.

"I didn't get all that much, you know. Nothing close to what you've prob'ly heard. Or for that matter nothing close to what I expected."

"I'm not a greedy man, Raider. Not terribly so, anyway. And I don't recall asking you how much you got from your robbery. The custom, which you probably would not know, is for the felon to make the exchange worthwhile for the operative by doubling his own reward. In your case, four thousand dollars."

Raider grinned and lowered his hands. MacDonald neither shot him nor protested. Neither, though, did the man remove any of the pressure he was applying with the muzzle of that .455.

"I don't suppose you'd negotiate," Raider said. "Since

we used to work together an' all."

"You're right. I don't suppose I would."

"Sure never knew you played that game, Donald."

MacDonald shrugged. "It's hardly the sort of thing to come up in casual conversation."

"Yeah, well, I might have some trouble coming up with four thousand cash money tonight."

"You aren't required to," MacDonald said. "The alternative, of course, is that I turn you in to the law. But the choice is certainly yours."

"You don't think I'd tell on you once I was behind bars anyway? Don't your other, uh, non-customers?"

"Actually," MacDonald said, "the problem has never arisen before. Those who suggest, shall we say, independent compensation only do so if they are able and willing to pay. Those who do not or cannot go routinely to jail for trial. I made an exception in your case because of our past association. The first time I have ever suggested it. I did think you might not understand the rules of the game. And of course you did not. Now you do."

"Interesting," Raider said. "So if I don't pay up, you cart me down the street and lock me up?"

"I would still get the two thousand in reward money."

"And you don't worry about me talking?"

MacDonald laughed. "I've never had any complaints before. Never. No one would take *your* word over mine."

Raider grinned at him. "Lucky for me Allan wants his revenge bad enough to make the reward offered for me alive only, ain't it?"

"I did think about that," MacDonald said. "In fact, I went to the trouble of verifying it this afternoon, after I saw you in the restaurant. If you want a really good disguise," MacDonald suggested, "you really should do something about the color of your hair and beard as well as..." He stopped talking abruptly, and his eyes widened.

"What's the matter, Donald?"

"You know more about disguise than that," MacDonald said. "You should have learned enough from Weatherbee to be able to do a better job than this."

"Yeah, well, we all make mistakes."

"I don't know." MacDonald sounded uncertain now, confused.

Raider could feel the pressure of the .455 muzzle increase. He thought MacDonald was about to cover himself at the expense of a $2,000 reward by pulling the trigger.

"Before you get too hasty," Raider said with a pretended calm, "you ought to know that my partner's standing right behind you."

MacDonald smiled. "Distraction, Raider? You aren't going to fool me that easily."

Raider grinned at him. "Yeah, well, it was worth the try."

Doc Weatherbee had had time to slip close enough now. Doc reached out and took hold of the Webley that was jammed into Raider's ribs.

MacDonald pulled the trigger, but the hammer could not fall into the primer in the brass end of the Webley cartridge. Doc's thumb had been laid between the hammer and backstrap of the stubby revolver.

Doc twisted and pulled the now harmless revolver out of MacDonald's hand, and Raider pulled back a rock-hard fist and coldcocked the Hodding operative.

MacDonald's knees sagged, and Raider hit him again, on the point of the chin this time. The man went out cold, like an ember hitting a mud puddle, and he dropped to the ground. Doc uncocked the Webley and stuck it in his coat pocket.

"What the hell are you doing here?" Raider asked. "I thought you were s'posed to be waiting for me over in Marcia's room."

"Grateful bastard, aren't you?"

"Oh, I ain't complaining. No, sir, I ain't."

"As a matter of fact," Doc said, "I came looking for you when you didn't show up on time. Interesting view in your room, I thought. You really should learn to pull your blinds."

Raider grinned at him. It was as much of a thank-you as Doc was likely to get.

"How much of that did you hear?" Raider asked.

"Enough," Doc said. "Enough to think we can't turn Mr. MacDonald loose or turn him over to his own agency. We'd be spilling the beans either way."

"Got any ideas?"

Doc fingered his chin for a moment and looked down at the unconscious form of the Hodding operative.

"I don't particularly like it, but I suppose we shall have to park the gentleman somewhere for a few days. Someplace out of the way. I know of an abandoned mine shaft we could use. But I don't know how often I could get away to feed and water him."

"His tough luck," Raider said. "Can you get him there by yourself?"

"He looks rather heavy."

"So we'll talk on the way an' take turns carryin' the son of a bitch." Raider bent over and with Doc's help got MacDonald balanced on his right shoulder. "If he comes to, bust 'im again," Raider said.

Doc led the way through the alleys toward the spot he had in mind. Behind him he could hear Raider chuckling.

"What's so funny?" he asked.

"I was just thinkin' how old Donald here is gonna wake up hoping you and me both survive this assignment. Be kinda hard on him if we was to be grassed."

"I suspect we will have his very best wishes," Doc agreed. "Now tell me about M. LeFarge and about that nymph you have stashed in your hotel room."

"You better watch yourself, Weatherbee," Raider said. "You already look like some kind o' degenerate. Next thing you know they'll have you in jail for charges of being a Peeping Tom."

# CHAPTER SEVENTEEN

"So," LeFarge said. "Our Mr. Jones appears to be genuine?"

Judith nodded. She licked her lips nervously. "He talks freely with me." Her eyes dropped away from LeFarge's. "I have guided the conversations the way you told me to. But subtly. He could not suspect. He talks about what his cut from the robbery should be and about . . . where he wants to take me afterward. The things he wants to do with me."

"Out of the bed also?" He laughed.

She nodded again. She was hoping with a desperation bordering on terror that LeFarge would not discover her lie. Amid the wonder of the discoveries she had begun to make with Raider, she had not once remembered to test him the way LeFarge had instructed her.

But she did not dare admit that to Charles. He had been rough with her in the past, even cruel. But he had always been careful to preserve her beauty and her body. He might not restrain himself if he discovered that she was not following his orders. And she had seen some of the terrible things he had done to other women from whom he wanted only short-term pleasures. Some of them would carry the scars of Charles LeFarge's "love making" for the rest of their pitiful lives. And those awful things he had done not in anger but simply for the pleasure their agony had given him.

Judith was petrified of LeFarge. She believed she had good reason to be.

Yet now she found herself lying to him for the very first time.

Two weeks ago, even two days ago, she could not have brought herself to do that. Somehow the feelings she was discovering with mysterious Raider were giving her the courage to thwart LeFarge's demands.

She wondered now if someday she might have the courage to leave LeFarge. If perhaps Raider himself might save her from him.

Although she had told LeFarge a lie about Raider wanting her to remain with him after this robbery, she was telling him more than a lie. She was telling him a fantasy as well, the one thing she could think of now that she might look forward to with hope and joy.

Perhaps, she thought wistfully, it was not really a lie. Perhaps it was only that these talks had not yet taken place.

She hoped that Raider would please and help Charles so much that LeFarge would suggest she stay with Raider. Or that Raider might like her so much that he might ask her to stay.

It didn't occur to her that she might change men of her own volition and will. During the past months LeFarge had dominated her so thoroughly that she no longer recognized any independent rights or desires she might once have possessed.

"You say you do not know where he went last night?" LeFarge asked.

She shook her head. "For a drink, I presume. He had it on his breath when he came back to the room."

"Where would he have gotten the money for that? Rolf took every last cent he had the other night."

Judith cringed away slightly but answered. "From me," she said. "He took money from my handbag. Not much. There was some."

LeFarge thought that over, then grunted. "All right, then. Just so that we do not find reason to suspect him."

"He had money," Judith repeated. "He smelled of liquor when he came back to my bed. I cannot tell you more than that."

LeFarge smiled, but there was no humor in it. The cruel twist at the corner of his mouth frightened her.

"You are keeping him blindly satisfied in the bed, eh, old girl?"

Judith's eyes fell, and she felt her shoulders tighten. "I am doing what you told me to do, Charles."

"Is our Mr. Jones good in bed, Judith? Does he fuck you thoroughly? Is he hung as well as I?"

"He is nothing like you, Charles," she said in perfect honesty. "But I think I satisfy him. You taught me everything I know."

The flattery seemed to please LeFarge. He motioned her closer. He was seated regally in the most comfortable chair of the suite while she stood nearby.

She moved to his side and remained still while he unfastened the buttons of her dress and slid both the dress and her chemise down to waist level, baring her breasts. His right hand cupped first one breast and then the other.

She found his touch repugnant. But that had become common over the past few months, after the first giddy excitement of being known by a man.

What startled her now was to discover that Charles's touch no longer aroused in her the stomach-wrenching thrill of guilty pleasure she also used to feel when he took her. Now, after the sweeter, softer, deeper pleasures of Raider, she no longer experienced that with Charles's touch. That was something she had not expected, something she was going to have to think about during the many long hours when she was alone with her thoughts.

Charles turned his hand and brushed her nipples with his knuckles. He didn't seem to notice that her nipples remained small and slack, not engorged this time with desire.

She knew better, though, than to try to pull away from him. He was smiling, and she could see a rising bulge at his fly. Her only thought was to hope that eagerness would make him finish quickly today.

Judith's salvation—and her shame—came in the form of a loud knocking at the door of the suite.

LeFarge allowed his hand to remain where it was as his attention went to the door. "Who?" he called out.

"Rolf."

"It's open."

Rolf came in and a smaller man with him. But then most men were smaller than Rolf. This one wore shabby trousers and no coat. His cuffs were held high by elastic sleeve garters. Judith had never seen him before.

She made no attempt to cover herself. Charles had not told her to do so.

Besides, Rolf already knew what she was like without her clothing. She looked at the big man with neither interest nor fear. He was brutally crude and direct, but when Charles chose to give her to Rolf the big man took her quickly, as a form of convenient release, like a man using a public outhouse.

It was the attention of the smaller man that embarrassed her. His eyes kept darting to her breasts and then away again, as if he wanted to stare but was afraid to. She noticed that he wore a wedding band on his left hand. It was rare to see any man who allowed himself to be publicly branded in that manner, and never had she seen it among Charles's company of men. It made her nervous now to be leered at by a man who belonged to another woman. She turned her head away and tried to pretend that she was alone in the room with Charles and Rolf.

"That fuckin' Raider ain't around?" Rolf asked.

"Sleeping," Charles explained. He smiled. "Judith tells me she is keeping him worn out."

Rolf grunted. He started to say something, but Charles cut him short.

"I will not forget. I promised. Now, what is it that makes you interrupt my morning?"

Rolf pointed toward the man who was with him. "Message come through. Thought you oughta know about it."

LeFarge turned to the smaller man, and at last he released his hand from Judith's breast. She wondered if Charles would mind if she covered herself, then decided against it. There was no point now in risking Charles's anger.

"Well, Robert?"

Robert looked at Judith and then away. "Another of those strange wires, boss. Something about an appropriation for an Operation Snare. The last time that was mentioned you seemed interested, so . . ."

"Yes, yes," LeFarge said impatiently. "Do you have a copy of the message for me?"

Robert looked unhappy. "No, sir. Harry was in the office with me, so I didn't have a chance to copy it down without him seeing."

LeFarge grunted and reached for a cigar. Judith held her dress up with one hand and hurried to get the nippers and a match for him.

"Tell me about it, then," LeFarge ordered.

"It was like that other one, sort of. From the boss of the Denver and Rio Grande to the, uh, let me see if I can remember it exactly, to the chief operating officer—that's the way it was addressed—at the Denver, South Park, and Pacific. It said a, uh, pro-rata share of the Operation Snare appropriation would be fourteen hundred dollars, payable immediately."

"It did not say anything about what this Operation Snare is?"

"No, sir. Not this time either."

"Or to whom the appropriation is payable?"

"No, sir. I'm sure of that."

"Hmmm," LeFarge mused. "Secrecy is not like them. Not at all."

"I been thinking about it, sir. Since that first message saying Operation Snare was starting."

"Yes?"

"The newspaper says there's another bunch of Russian royalty on a hunting trip up around Yellowstone. You know. Buffalo and like that. Could be they want to come down here and take a special train up into the mountains for elk or something."

LeFarge glared at Robert. "A simple thing like that would not require secrecy and code names. Besides, they are paid for special trains. The railroads do not pay others for the priviledge of serving them. Not even nobility." He looked at Judith and laughed. "Correct, my dear?"

She blushed. Perhaps the most foolish mistake she had ever made was to tell Charles about the title she had been born to. "Yes, Charles," she whispered.

"I'm sorry I don't know more, but..."

LeFarge waved the clerk away. "I want to find out more about this Operation Snare, Robert. See if you can learn anything."

"Yes, sir."

"And Robert."

"Yes?"

"If you do learn anything, you shall be paid very well. Think about that, Robert. Now you may go. You too, Rolf. I don't want you around when Raider wakes up. We still need him, and I know I can't ask but so much of your self control. Go on now."

"Yes, sir."

The two men left the suite, and Charles began undoing the buttons at his fly.

# CHAPTER EIGHTEEN

Raider woke to a wet sound he could not identify. He plumped the pillow behind his neck and pushed with his legs so he was sitting up against the headboard. He watched with pleasure as Judith finished gargling and then scrubbed at her teeth with baking soda from a small jar beside the basin.

Her hair was down and gleamed from being freshly brushed. She was wearing a light dressing gown. As she moved, it became obvious that it was the only garment she had on.

"Nice," he said.

"Oh!" She jumped, startled, then turned to him with a smile. "I thought you were asleep yet."

"Lazy is what you mean, and you're right."

"You must have been tired last night. You never moved when I got up earlier."

He raised an eyebrow.

"I am quite ahead of you. Been down the hall for a bath so I'm nice and fresh for you." She laid her toothbrush aside and wiped her mouth with a small towel provded by the hotel, then came to curl up beside him on the bed.

She smelled of soap and toilet water. Raider untied the cloth belt of the dressing gown and flipped the gown open so he could admire the long, sleek curves of her.

"Nice," he repeated.

"Do you think so? Truly?"

His answer was to take her in his arms and roll her across his body so that she lay tucked in against his right side. He kissed her, enjoying the play of her tongue against his.

He bent to take one firm nipple between his lips and rolled it back and forth with the tip of his tongue. Judith began to moan.

Wantonly she reached for his hand and guided it to the scant patch of fluff between her parted legs.

He moistened a fingertip in the honeypot she provided for him there and ran the wet finger up to the small bump of her clitoris. He rubbed her lightly, alternating the gentle strokes with equally gentle flicks of his nail against that most sensitive area.

Judith's breath came heavier and quicker. "Yes, darling, yes." She arched her hips and opened her legs wider, giving him access to her body, demanding that he use that access.

Raider smiled and nipped lightly at the firm, pink nipple between his teeth.

She cried out and climaxed with convulsive sobs, clamping her thighs tight around his hand and trapping him there.

At last she came drifting back from wherever her ecstasy had taken her. She smiled and pressed her hand against his cheek, drawing him up so she could kiss him. She sighed.

"I am ever so grateful," she whispered. "Did you know that, darling?"

Raider's answer was a smile.

She reached between their bodies and found his cock. It was already erect. She ran her fingertips up and down its length with obvious joy, then reached lower to cup and tease his balls.

She ran her hand back up his shaft and toyed with the small slit at the tip end, then down again so she could grasp him and begin rolling his foreskin gently up and down.

"Careful," he said. "Wouldn't want to waste it."

With a giggle of sheer delight, Judith scooted lower on the broad, soft bed and parted her legs wide for him. She tugged lightly on his cock, pulling him into position over her.

She guided the head of his cock to the wet, eager entry and sighed with pleasure when he braced himself above her and remained poised there, barely inside her. With both hands she caressed and tantalized his shaft and balls while the head of his marble-hard penis rested just inside her.

Slowly Raider lowered himself. He slid easily into the warm depths of her while Judith continued to massage his balls and what she could reach of his shaft.

When he was socketed fully inside her, engulfed by the heat of her body and soothed by the welcoming wetness she offered him, she took her hands away and wrapped her arms and legs tight around him, clinging to him and tilting her pelvis to receive the last fraction of an inch from his exceptional length.

With a low, teasing chuckle, Raider came to his knees and maneuvered carefully to the side of the bed.

He stood, and Judith was still locked tight around him with her arms and long, slender thighs. He remained deep inside her as he stood.

He took one cheek of her ass in each hand to help support her weight. Faking a yawn he walked to the window and looked out. Bright sunshine in an almost cloudless sky told him he had slept very nearly until noon after the long chore of helping Weatherbee stash a protesting Donald Mac-Donald in an unused mine tunnel.

Not, however, that he was thinking about that at the moment.

He looked down at Judith, and she raised her face to him for a lingering kiss.

He went back to the bed and leaned over it, lowering her to it and continuing down until his weight was taken on her pelvic bones.

He let go of her rump and leaned back so he could grasp her legs behind the knees and push them forward, bending her nearly double with her legs extended up over her shoulders.

"I'm not hurting you, am I?"

She shook her head quickly, a happy smile on her face. "I've never done this before, luv. It lets me feel you all the deeper inside me."

"Uh huh. That's the idea, honey."

Slowly he began to stroke in and out, moving only a little at first, then gradually lengthening his strokes until he was nearly pulling free of her at the end of each partial withdrawl.

"Oh, my," Judith said breathlessly.

Raider laughed. He was enjoying himself. She seemed to be enjoying it too.

"I can't reach you," he instructed, "so take one hand and touch yourself for me."

"Should I?"

"Of course."

She did as she was told, and soon her eyes lost their focus and her expression was loose and dreamy.

She quickly learned to stroke herself in time to his thrusts.

Raider began to move quicker, and so did she.

As the rising pressure in his balls built toward the bursting point, he lost his slow, careful control and began to thrust and batter into her in a frenzy.

He was only dimly aware of Judith's cry of release, but the sudden constriction of her pussy around the shaft of his cock was enough to send him spurting and heaving over the final brink of pleasure, and he plunged forward into her while he pumped gouts of hot fluid deep inside her.

He collapsed on top of her and lay there for a moment.

Then, with a muttered "Damn," he pulled away.

"Is something wrong?"

"No, I . . . thought I must be hurting you. Bent up like a pretzel and all."

She laughed and uncurled from the tucked-up position she had been in. "I enjoyed it. Truly."

"Good."

Raider rolled aside and came into a sitting position on the side of the bed. He looked at her and shook his head. "I swear I don't know how you manage to look so cool and fresh after all that."

"Last night you were accusing me of sweating, dearest."

"I lied."

Judith kissed him and slid down until she was sitting on the carpet at his feet. She touched him, taking his limp, satiated cock onto her fingers. With her other hand she pulled his foreskin back. She leaned closer and peered at him as if looking at a man's tool for the very first time, inspecting and admiring it.

"Yes?" he asked.

"D'you mind?"

"Not at all."

"Good." She continued to look at him, raising and lowering his flaccid cock so she could inspect it from all angles.

Then, unexpectantly, she bent forward and took him into her mouth. She caressed him with her tongue and rolled his cock from one side of her mouth to the other.

"What the hell are you doing?"

"He was sticky, luv. Can't let the darlin' boy stay all sticky and used-up looking, can we now?"

Raider laughed.

Judith looked up at him, his limp pecker hanging out of the corner of her mouth, and winked.

"You silly damn wench."

On the other hand, possibly not so silly. He was already growing again, each heartbeat sending a fresh flow of blood pumping into his cock to stiffen and strengthen it.

Raider reached down to take her by the shoulders and

lift her onto the bed at his side. He rolled on top of her and once again allowed her to guide him where they both thought he should be.

She pumped her hips beneath him, encouraging him to move faster and deeper and drawing him higher and higher into a whirlagig spiral of sensation.

Raider lay sweaty and exhausted on the sour sheets of the hotel bed. He damned sure hoped the management was going to provide clean sheets today. If they didn't, the room was soon going to smell like a cathouse the morning after payday.

"Hungry?" he asked.

"Not really."

"You eat less than any person I ever come across before."

Judith smiled at him. "What I just had, darling, satisfies me much more than food possibly could."

"I think I'll take that as a compliment, ma'am."

"Please do, sir. And please as well feed me in that fashion as often as possible."

"My pleasure, ma'am."

Her smile faded, and she looked serious. "Do you know Charles's man Rolf, dearest?"

Raider thought for a moment, then shook his head. "I haven't met any of LeFarge's bunch, and I can't remember knowin' anybody named Rolf."

"I . . . ran into Charles this morning. When I went out for my bath. Rolf was with him. I got the impression that Rolf does not like you. He worries me."

Raider shrugged. "There's plenty that don't like me, honey. What were they talkin' about?"

He was asking why she thought this Rolf did not like him, but Judith misunderstood. And this time, in the afterglow of the pleasure Raider had given her, she didn't think to be afraid of what Charles might do to her later.

"Charles was worried," she said truthfully. "About something called Operation Snare."

Raider felt a cold chill rise up his spine. He sat bolt

upright, startling Judith. "Are you sure about that?"

Operation Snare was the code name that had been given to this assignment. And only six people in the whole damned world were supposed to know it.

How in hell had Charles LeFarge come by that knowledge? And what *else* did he know?

Raider grabbed for his clothes and began pulling them on.

The morning had been fun and all that, but he wished to hell Judith had told him about this earlier.

# CHAPTER NINETEEN

Doc glanced nervously toward the sky. Not that there was anything wrong with it. It was a beautiful day. But there was not all that much day left now, and Doc had more on his plate at the moment than he could comfortably handle.

There was, of course, the question of protecting Raider. That, after all, was the primary reason Doc was here. It was his responsibility to see to it that Raider lived to complete the assignment. It would be rather nice as well if Raider were to live beyond it.

There was also now the necessity to take food and water to Donald MacDonald, their captive competitor from the Hodding Agency. The man had been in the old mine tunnel now for half the night and nearly all of today, and he was undoubtedly hungry, thirsty, and smelling rank. Handcuffs and a foraged length of logging chain made sure MacDonald could not get out to fend for his own needs, which placed them squarely on Weatherbee's well-padded shoulders for the time being. For just how long, Doc could not guess but certainly for the next several days, until the gold shipment was scheduled to take place.

And finally there was now a pressing need to confer with at least one of the railroad principals who had hired them for Operation Snare.

Doc sat on a broken crate and took a sip of strong tea from a washed and re-used pint whiskey bottle. The tea was refreshing, and its container should help add to his cover story if anyone happened to be watching. He took another sip and thought about what Raider had told him.

Damn the man anyway. He had taken too great a chance contacting Doc during daylight hours when they might have been observed.

But, Doc admitted to himself, he very likely would have done the same thing if their positions had been reversed. Information like that the girl had given Raider simply had to be passed along.

They had to find out whether Operation Snare had been compromised and—equally important—just how Charles LeFarge was receiving such extremely sensitive information. Determining that, Doc believed, would be half their battle in stopping LeFarge.

Doc thought it over, but the conclusion he came to seemed inescapable.

Raider was more than merely competent at defending himself. He would just have to watch his own backside until Doc could get down to Denver and work on the most important of the duties he now faced.

As for MacDonald, the man would just have to grit his teeth and wait for Weatherbee's return. He wouldn't be comfortable, but he would survive long enough to face the humiliation of being exposed before his peers. Doc doubted that MacDonald would ever actually be prosecuted for his bribe taking, but at least he could expect dismissal from the Hodding Agency and blackballing from the Pinkerton Agency and all the pretenders to the Pinkerton throne.

And Doc, of course, would have to make his way as quickly as possible down to Denver.

There was no choice but for him to make the trip in person. According to what the girl had told Raider, the man named Robert had told LeFarge that the message was contained in a wire. Therefore Doc was forced to conclude that it would not be safe for him to send a telegraph message, even in code.

Not that travelling down to Denver should present any great problems, unless something unexpected took place up here in Leadville. The gold was not scheduled for shipment for another two days.

There was a southbound train making up at the Denver & Rio Grande yard now. Doc could ride it as far as Buena Vista and connect there with a Denver, South Park & Pacific through Garo, Red Hill, and Como, and finally on to Denver.

He should be in Denver before morning, and back in Leadville before nightfall tomorrow with ample time then to check on Raider, tend to MacDonald, and get ready for the final, critical period when the gold was being transported.

So far Raider had no idea how LeFarge intended to take the gold shipment, but the man was certain to have something devious up his sleeve.

Sometime between now and the actual shipment time it was Raider's job to discover LeFarge's plan and get the information out so Doc could thwart it.

No point in worrying about that now, Doc thought. Worrying would not help either one of them.

Doc tucked his "whiskey" bottle into a side pocket of his coat and staggered erect. In his ponderous, old-man's gait he ambled along the tracks toward the cars that were being made up into the southbound train.

He regretted having to leave Raider here with no backup, but they had no choice. Damn it.

Doc shuffled along beside one of the freight cars that was being deadheaded back toward Pueblo. He glanced around to make sure no one was paying attention to him, then dropped onto his belly and with monkey-like agility slipped under the frame of the empty car and up onto the rods.

He curled up there and made himself as comfortable as possible.

He sighed. Travel like this gave him some measure of respect for, but absolutely no envy whatsoever of, the hoboes who routinely rode the rods the length and breadth of the country.

He waited patiently for the engine to shackle on and begin the downhill run toward Buena Vista.

# CHAPTER TWENTY

"Darling."

"Yes?" Raider was interrupted in the unpleasant but necessary chore of trying to brush his coat and trousers back into some semblance of respectability. Not having a change of clothing was beginning to become as bothersome as not having a hat. He intended to ask LeFarge for some of that spending money the man had promised.

Judith closed the door behind her but did not lock it. "Charles wants to see you, dear. At once, he said."

"All right." Raider pulled on his pants but left the coat draped over the back of the chair.

"You shall probably want your coat this time," Judith said. She took a bonnet from the wardrobe and tied the ribbons under her chin. Or a hat or chapeau or whatever the hell she wanted to call it, Raider thought. Something that fancy would probably not be known as a bonnet.

"Why so dandy?" he asked.

"He will meet us south of town along the river. I have rented horses waiting outside."

Raider shrugged and put his coat on. He wondered why the mystery all of a sudden but was not in a position to quarrel.

He escorted Judith downstairs and through the lobby of the hotel to the tie rail out front where a pair of typically cobby-looking livery horses were waiting. As saddle horses, Raider thought, either one of them would make decent bear bait. One carried a much used rimfire stock saddle, the other an old but well-cared-for sidesaddle. He gave Judith a hand up and held the horse she had been given until she was as firmly seated as was possible in the sidesaddle rig, then swung onto the other horse.

She led the way south past the business district and the surrounding mines and stamp mills of busy Leadville, then annoyed the livery horse with her heel until she convinced the animal to take a slow canter.

She rode well, Raider observed. As naturally and well as a Texan, in spite of the silliness of the sidesaddle. A woman who could accomplish that, he had always thought, was something special. Ask most any man to ride like that and the son of a bitch would be pulling dirt out of his ears in no time, but a frail female was expected to handle it as a matter of course.

A couple of miles south of Leadville Judith slowed their pace and guided the horse off the road to the left, across rugged, rocky terrain and down toward the Arkansas River, which was practically foaming here with leaping, white water just as rugged as the rocks along its shore. As they neared the river, its noise surrounded them, making conversation difficult although not impossible.

"Are you sure you know where you're going?" Raider had to lean forward in his saddle and raise his voice to make himself heard over the noise of the river.

Judith did not try to answer except to nod. It was easier than speaking. Raider followed obediently.

They reached the rocky bank of the swift-running river and turned left, back toward Leadville.

With summer well advanced and the spring flooding past its peak, there was a stretch of dry rock and gravel on both sides of the river that was twenty or more yards wide.

Steep walls farther upstream showed where the channel had been cut during the highest flow of the mighty river, which took its head somewhere above Leadville and thundered through mountains and plains for probably a thousand miles before it finally reached the Mississippi.

They rounded one of the river's ten thousand curves, and Raider finally understood.

From the road they had not been able to see the dry bank beneath the rocky cut on the west side of the Arkansas.

Charles LeFarge was waiting there. So were probably eighteen heavily armed men.

Their horses were tied to makeshift rails fashioned from pieces of driftwood. The men were taking their ease, some sitting on the larger boulders that littered the flat riverbank, others gathered with cards or dice around horse blankets that had been spread over the gravel. Two of the men had taken lengths of cord and were fishing in the rapid water with no apparent success.

LeFarge stood when he saw them approach. Beside him another man stood—an exceptionally tall and well-built man with a full beard and a pair of Smith and Wesson revolvers in his belt.

Raider dismounted and helped Judith down from her horse. "What's up?" he asked LeFarge.

"You don't know?"

"I wouldn't have asked you if I already knew," Raider returned. They had to stand close together and speak loudly in order to be heard. The rapids nearby were so bad they made the river look like it was boiling. Raider was sure neither Judith nor LeFarge's companion could hear what was said.

LeFarge reached into his pocket and pulled out a folded sheet of paper. It was a telegraph message form, filled out in a spidery hand that belonged to a man who either had remarkably poor penmanship or had been in one hell of a hurry to write the message.

"No report Operation Snare," the message read. "Advance shipment schedule 48 hours."

"Son of a bitch," Raider said.

"What was the original schedule?" LeFarge asked.

Raider wondered briefly if this might be a trick of LeFarge's to force Raider to tell him when the gold was supposed to move. He looked past the man, toward the members of LeFarge's gang, and decided that, no, LeFarge would not have brought them all together like this for a trick. The man had been keeping them too well hidden before.

"Day after tomorrow," Raider said. "Leaving at ten o'clock. That would give them time to load after dark and make the transfer before dawn. Like I told you before, instead of going the expected route and transferring to a westbound at Buena Vista, they figured to go all the way down to Pueblo and then north, all the way out to Julesburg, before they put the gold onto a westbound at the Union Pacific main line. They figured that would avoid the most vulnerable grade in Monarch Pass and get by any likely robbery plan."

LeFarge nodded. He gave Raider a hard look, then smiled. "So," he said. "You have been telling me the truth."

Raider raised an eyebrow.

"I have a well-paid friend who is a guard at the Queen of Sheba mine. He knows little, but what he does know he tells accurately. Early this afternoon, not long after this wire was intercepted, he was told he would have to work late tonight taking the Queen of Sheba's portion of the gold shipment to the rail yard."

"Damn," Raider said. He looked at the message form again. "What's this Operation Snare thing?"

"I was hoping you could tell me that, my friend."

Raider shook his head. "Whatever it is it happened after I, uh" he grinned—"parted company with the Pinks."

LeFarge gestured with his hand as if he were shoving something out of the way. "Whatever," he said, "it seems that it has failed. All the better for us, yes?"

"Yes," Raider agreed. But inside he was groaning. Weatherbee was nowhere around now that he was needed. And with no more firepower of his own than a damned seven-shot .22 muff gun, Raider had a suspicion that he would not do so well taking on LeFarge's entire crew by his lonesome.

This was what happened when a man depended on careful, complicated planning, Raider thought ruefully. It all turned into a pile of crap.

"What do we do now?" Raider asked.

LeFarge smiled. He looked pleased with himself, even smug.

"Thanks to my good partner," LeFarge said, tapping Raider on the chest, "I shall not make the expected mistakes." He grinned. "By the by, my dear man, I compliment you on your security arrangements. They would have been most effective against any ordinary plan."

"That's what I thought," Raider agreed, "so I hope you got something in mind that ain't ordinary."

"My intentions are the essence of simplicity, Mr. Raider," LeFarge said with pleasure. "Four miles to the south of here there is a small bridge spanning a creek bed. The creek runs only in the spring. It is dry at this time of year."

"I remember it from the maps when I was doing the planning for the shipment," Raider said. "There's another of those north o' here and three more between that one an' Buena Vista."

"Exactly. Your memory is excellent," LeFarge said with satisfaction. "The bridge to the south is the highest of the five, yes?"

Raider shrugged. "The map didn't show nothing about how high any of them was."

"Trust me," LeFarge said. "This one, it is the highest of them all."

"So?"

"So it is very simple. During the late afternoon, by ones and twos, my men and I cross to the far side of the river on the suspension bridges closer to Leadville."

Raider remembered those, too. There were several of them. They served the work crews in the stamp mills that had been built on the outskirts of Leadville.

"We travel down to the bridge, eh? We carry a box of this, a smattering of that." He was smiling. "When the correct train approaches the bridge"—he made a shoving motion with his hands, like a man pushing forcefully down on a blaster's magneto-powered battery box—"boom! No more bridge. The train falls conveniently to the floor of the dry creek bed. Your so heavily armed guards, they should be killed. Any who are not shall be in no condition to fight. The crates of gold, they can be picked up like so many pebbles on a bare path."

Raider was appalled by the loss of life LeFarge intended, but he did not dare show it. He forced himself to smile. Then he looked worried.

"Yes?" LeFarge asked.

"You're leavin' out a few minor details," Raider said. "Like what the hell do you do with all that gold once you got it. Man, I've checked that country east o' the tracks. There's no horse gonna cross it, an' it would take a whole damn army to pack it out on their backs. I mean, you got one hell of a lot of bulk an' weight to that much gold, Charles."

LeFarge was still smiling. "Again, my friend, simplicity is the answer. All this past week my men have been constructing rafts. They are complete and waiting, hidden in the dry creek bed away from the river. We gather the gold and place the crates on the rafts. The river does the work of carrying them down. The worst of the rapids are here. Also below where we need the rafts. We float the gold down. Already there are men waiting for us with mules. Or they shall be by the time we need them. The mules and packs are assembled. They need only to be told that it is tonight they must meet us. We load the gold onto the mules.

More mules than we actually need, of course. We travel south and west, around Buena Vista. Lay a false trail through Monarch Pass and take our gold safely south through Poncha Pass and into the San Luis Valley. No one could ever find us once we reach the San Luis." LeFarge laughed. "Besides, they shall all be chasing us through Monarch. Which you yourself tell me they expect us to run. How do you think of it, eh?"

Raider grinned at him. "Charles," he said, "I am damned glad that you and me are partners instead o' the other way around on this one. I do believe you're gonna make me an awful rich man before the next daylight."

"Exactly," LeFarge said. "Exactly." He turned and said something to the tall man who was still standing behind him, then leaned forward and beckoned Judith closer.

"Go back to my suite and wait for me," he told her. "I have great plans for you tomorrow. Then, my sweet, if you wish, you may rejoin Mr. Raider. I shall want you no more."

Raider thought that Judith looked pale at the thought of what Charles LeFarge might have planned for her in the aftermath of his largest robbery. The celebration apparently was not something she was looking forward to.

But she did as she was told. Raider helped her onto her sidesaddle, and she rode back the way they had just come. She looked around just once and gave Raider a sad, wistful smile.

# CHAPTER TWENTY-ONE

The sun was already below the range of jagged mountains to the west. High overhead the sky was still bright, but in the shadow of the mountains dusk had come. It would be some time yet before it was fully dark.

LeFarge and the big man went back to join the others. Raider tethered his nag—appearance and performance alike justified the term—with the rest of the horses and walked to the edge of the river.

He stared at the foaming white water for several minutes. It was no wonder the men who were fishing had not caught anything. Surely nothing, not even a fish, could live in water that turbulent.

The water surged downhill with awesome force, leaping high into the air every time it encountered the obstruction of a rock. And there were a great many sharp-edged rocks in the riverbed here.

Raider saw a length of driftwood spin through the rough water. It danced and leaped, being flung from one boulder to the next. By the time it exited the rapids into slightly calmer water below, it had been broken and splintered and reduced to less than half the size it had been when Raider first saw it.

Raider was watching the driftwood float out of sight when he felt a touch at his left shoulder. He spun, his hand instinctively snaking toward the butt of a Colt revolver he no longer was carrying.

He stopped when he saw that it was LeFarge. He had not been able to hear the man's approach over the sound of the river. As before, the tall, heavily built man was beside him.

LeFarge leaned forward. This close to the river he practically had to shout into Raider's ear to make himself heard.

"Time to go notify the men with the mules," he yelled. "I want you to go with my man Rolf. I shall take charge here. Rolf is to be in charge with the mules. You understand?"

"I'd rather stay an' be part of the heist," Raider said.

"This I did not ask, my friend. You go with Rolf now. We will join you with the gold by midnight. No later. You take your share then if you wish."

"It ain't that I don't trust you, damn it. I just wanta be in on it."

"My men work well together. They know what they are to do. You would only be in the way," LeFarge insisted.

Raider looked past LeFarge's shoulder. Rolf's expression was threatening, as if he for one would welcome argument.

"Whatever you say, partner," Raider said.

LeFarge nodded, then turned and said something into Rolf's ear. Raider could see LeFarge's lips move, but he could make out no sound over the roar of the rapids.

Raider could remember Judith telling him something about a man named Rolf. He could not recall exactly what it was she had said, but he had the impression it had been something unpleasant.

And there was the description the badly injured guard

had given after the South Texas train robbery. The leader of the gang could have been this Rolf.

Come to think of it, Raider realized, Charles LeFarge had never been known to actually participate in any of the robberies he had planned. Was he going to make an exception this time? Or was something else going on here?

Raider smiled and shook Rolf's hand, then followed as the big man went to the horses and tightened the cinch of a leggy, fine-looking bay. Raider's livery stable jughead was all the poorer in comparison with Rolf's mount. Raider pulled his cinches snug and mounted.

There was no point in attempting conversation here even if he had felt any desire to do so, which he did not. He followed docilely behind as Rolf led the way downriver, holding to the nearly flat bank immediately beside the Arkansas. The going would have been much easier up on the road, of course, but Rolf probably didn't want to be seen.

Raider glanced over his shoulder before they rounded the curve out of sight of the waiting gang. It was nearly dusk now, and LeFarge was assembling the men. Some of them were beginning to move toward their horses. They were going to have a long walk from the lowest suspension bridge to the ambush site, Raider thought. LeFarge was probably moving them into position already.

The miserable, ugly, coarse-boned jughead saved Raider's life—the horse and the fact that Rolf didn't want simply to kill Raider; the man apparently wanted to maim him first.

Raider had been glancing down toward the rapids they were passing. He had thought the rapids up above had been bad. These were even worse, and he was fascinated by them.

He looked down toward the foaming water, mesmerized by its fury and its power.

His horse shied violently to the side, and only Raider's years in the saddle kept him from spilling off onto the jagged rocks they were traveling over.

He moved swiftly and automatically with the horse, maintaining his balance by feel, and a clubbed fist swept harmlessly past his ear.

While Raider had been looking away toward the river,

Rolf had slowed his bay to let Raider come up beside him. He swung his left fist in a vicious, backhanded arc that would have knocked Raider from the saddle—and probably would have knocked him unconscious as well—but the livery stable horse saw the sudden motion and shied away from it. Probably the horse's unpleasant existence had taught it to expect and to be shy of punishment. But whatever the reason, the horse darted to the side, and Raider jerked his head around in time to see Rolf's fist pass.

Raider pulled on his reins, trying to make the jughead spin away from Rolf and his bay, but this time the horse let him down. It stumbled and went to its knees.

Raider thought the beast was going all the way down. He kicked free of his stirrups and jumped clear.

Without Raider's weight to contend with, the livery horse regained its feet and trotted a few yards away to the edge of the high-water channel where it found some weeds to browse.

Raider stood with his hands on his hips in disgust, glaring first at the treacherous horse and then at a grinning Rolf who sat on his tall bay and laughed.

Once again Raider's hand swept automatically toward the Colt he should have been wearing, but there was nothing there. Rolf saw and began to laugh harder. Raider showed him an extended middle finger and began looking on the ground for a rock of throwing size. If he was going to have to face down a man wearing two revolvers and himself barehanded...

Rolf grinned at him again and dismounted. He seemed in no hurry about it. He unbuckled the near pouch of his saddlebags and glanced over his shoulder to make sure Raider was watching. Then, slowly and with pleasure, he removed both Smiths from his waistband and tucked them into the saddlebags.

He carefully buckled the bag shut again and looked back toward Raider with a smile, forming his huge hands into fists and holding them up for Raider to see.

This time Raider grinned back at him. If that was the way the man wanted it . . .

Rolf took his time also about removing his vest and shirt. He flexed his muscles and studied Raider's face for a re- action.

Silly son of a bitch, Raider thought. Probably expected to win fights by making the other fellow drop away into a dead faint from sheer terror.

The bastard was, Raider admitted, built as least as well as an average ox.

He was slightly taller than Raider and considerably heav- ier. And there didn't seem to be an ounce of spare flesh on him.

His upper body was hairless and gleamed as though it had been oiled. Slabs of muscle corded his belly and chest, and his bicep muscles rolled and heaved like separate live things beneath the skin.

Shee-it, Raider thought. No wonder the bastard looked and acted so almighty confident.

On the other hand, a great many men who have physical power lack the knowledge of how to use it. And Raider had come through many and many a rough-and-tumble brawl in his time. More than he would care to count now. If Rolf did not know how to use his strength . . .

Uh oh, Raider told himself.

Rolf came forward, toward him. But the big man was not just walking along. He moved with fluid grace, never allowing himself to be in any way out of balance. And the damn man was carrying his fists high, cocked in the ap- proved stance Raider had seen so many times in professional prizefight rings.

As he came closer, Rolf began to shuffle forward, his left foot always slightly in advance of the right. He looked as light on his feet as a good cutting horse.

Yeah, Raider thought, he knew what he was doing.

Rolf stopped and said something, but Raider could not hear and shook his head.

Rolf looked around on the ground for a moment and spotted a small, gray twig that had been left behind when the Arkansas receded after the spring flooding. He picked it up and held it between his two hands to snap it. Then he looked at Raider and grinned.

The implication was clear enough. He intended to break Raider the same way he had just broken the twig.

Looking at him, Raider suspected the SOB was capable of doing just that.

Raider shrugged and stuck his hands in his pockets. Rolf took one of the pieces of twig and broke it again, as if to say that he was going to break Raider's back whether Raider resisted or not.

That, however, was not what Raider had in mind.

And, hell, this was not some prizefight where judges would decide if a fellow had followed the rules or not. Besides, a broken back could ruin a man's whole day.

Raider pulled the tiny .22 from his coat pocket, cocked and fired it into Rolf's massive chest.

Oh, *shit!* Raider thought.

A dot not much larger than a freckle appeared on one of the bulging muscles. That and an expression of fury on the big man's face was the only reaction the pipsqueak bullet got.

Raider glared down at the little gun. Its report had barely been heard over the sound of the river, and he recalled now that the extremely short cartridges for those little guns were propelled only by the rimfire primer and a few grains of powder.

Rolf, thoroughly pissed off, judging from his expression, began to come forward again.

Raider gave Rolf an apologetic smile and shot him again. And then again. And yet again until the little bitty gun ran dry.

Seven undersized slugs, and it looked like not more than two or maybe three of them had done much more than penetrate Rolf's hide.

There was not even any blood to show for it all.
Rolf was too close for comfort now.
Raider turned and ran like hell.

# CHAPTER TWENTY-TWO

The son of a bitch was big. He was also quick. Raider feinted a dash toward his own miserable horse, then darted instead for Rolf's handsome bay—and for the pair of Smith and Wesson .44s in that saddlebag. One good slug from a .44—Raider took another look—okay, *two* well-placed .44 slugs and Rolf would be down for the count for the last time.

But Rolf shifted direction easily in spite of the uncertain, rocky footing and made a lunge for Raider that snagged the edge of Raider's sleeve.

Raider jerked his arm away and set out in a dead run up the river-bank. Rolf was right behind.

Raider sprinted hard for a hundred yards or so, Rolf still within half a dozen feet of him, and then stretched his legs like a Blackfoot with half a dozen Sioux hot on his ass.

Raider thought he was gaining some ground finally. He glanced over his shoulder. Sure enough, Rolf was ten yards behind now, and the distance was still growing.

"Shit!"

Raider went down. The side of his foot had hit the edge of a rock and slipped off, twisting his ankle and destroying his balance.

Raider tucked his head under and rolled with the force of his forward motion, turning a somersault and coming back onto his feet almost immediately.

Unfortunately, "almost" was not good enough. Rolf had had time to close the distance.

The big man threw himself on top of Raider, arms outstretched, face contorted with fury.

The impact of Rolf's body landing on his exploded the air from Raider's lungs, but he had no time to worry about small things like that. He twisted and rolled, eeling out from under Rolf and throwing himself to the side before Rolf could get a grip on him. Rolf scrambled after him, both men on hands and knees.

Raider was still off balance. Since he had no time to change that fact, he tried to turn it to his advantage. He fell backward, landing hard on his back, and drew his knees up into a fetal position.

As soon as Rolf scrambled within range, Raider lashed out with both feet, driving the heels of his boots into the man's jaw.

The force of that kick should have been enough to kill any normal human being. It stopped Rolf, rocking him backward and bringing a flow of blood from his mouth, but he only shook his head and came forward again.

At least the momentary pause gave Raider time enough to gulp in a deep breath. He crabbed backward on the ground and came to his feet.

Rolf lunged for him again. Again Raider's boot snaked forward. The boot caught Rolf on the temple and ripped forward, nearly tearing the man's ear off.

Rolf shook his head, and his blood splattered Raider's coat.

"We could discuss this, you know," Raider reasoned.

Rolf probably couldn't hear the words over the loud rush of the river, but he might have guessed their intent. He grinned at Raider and shook his head. Then he started forward again.

Both men were moving more slowly now than they had been. Raider's ribs had been reinjured when Rolf landed on him, and he was having difficulty breathing.

As for Rolf, Raider didn't know what in hell kept him coming after those kicks to the head. Son of a bitch oughta be dead, Raider told himself.

And shot seven times in the belly besides that. Lordy!

Raider backed away.

He felt a soft, insistent pull at his boots. Only then did he realize that sometime during all of that, Rolf had managed to maneuver him so that Raider's back was to the river and Rolf was between him and the safety of solid ground.

Raider took another half step backward. He was in water past his ankles now, and the river bed sloped sharply under his feet.

The roar of the surging, white water seemed all the louder when he realized that.

The footrace had taken them upstream, to the start of the rapids Raider had been marveling at when Rolf jumped him. Downstream from here the river was a solid boil of foam and rock.

Raider looked again. No one, but no one, could hope to swim across that. The current was too strong, the rocks too many and entirely too deadly.

He looked back at Rolf, and the big man grinned. He knew Raider's dilemma. He was enjoying it.

Raider crouched at the river's edge. He squatted and waited, one hand trailing in the cold water, while Rolf took several deep breaths and flexed his muscles to test them and pump fresh blood into them.

The bastard was still grinning.

He took a step forward, and Raider straightened.

Raider came up with a rock the size of a grapefruit in his fist. He didn't give Rolf time to duck or to dart aside but tossed the stone in a quick, underhand throw.

Rolf blinked and tried to back away, but he had not recognized the threat in time.

The rock caught him just above the bridge of his nose, breaking the nose and splitting the skin. He was still bleeding from the mouth and the ear. Now this fresh wound gushed blood as well.

Raider tried to run, but the pull of the racing river water at his feet slowed him.

Rolf's mouth opened in a bellow of rage that Raider could see but could not even faintly hear.

Blinded by the flow of blood, arms held wide and searching, Rolf lunged forward.

Raider tried to duck away from him, but one ham-sized fist closed on Raider's shoulder.

Raider felt himself being swept into a bloody bear hug against Rolf's massive chest.

Rolf's arms clamped down like a blacksmith's vise, and Raider could feel white-hot pain shoot through his already damaged ribs, as though a smith's superheated mandrel had been shoved inside his body.

A few more seconds of this, Raider knew, and Rolf would kill him for sure.

Raider had no leverage and no time. He had to do something *now*.

He threw himself backward, taking Rolf with him.

Raider felt the sharp drop of the riverbed under his boots, and he shoved back with all the strength he had.

Icy, foaming water closed over them both, and, still locked in Rolf's crushing grip, Raider and his enemy were spun toward the roaring torrent of the white-water rapids.

# CHAPTER TWENTY-THREE

Charles LeFarge was thoroughly pissed off, although that was not the way he would have phrased it in the elegant French he affected at such times.

It was already well past full darkness, and the last of the men were filtering silently into position around the dry gully where soon the gold-laden train would crash. In that respect everything was going nicely.

What annoyed LeFarge was the Rolf was overdue. Solid, trustworthy (LeFarge still found that to be incredible, and in its own way amusing, but after all this time the hulking and dependable Rolf had been tested time and time again; he was unfailingly trustworthy) Rolf was late.

Not that LeFarge foresaw any real difficulty with Rolf's disposal of the former Pinkerton operative known alternately as Raider or as Mr. Jones.

Rolf could handle Raider and half a carload just like him without raising a sweat.

What LeFarge suspected was that the damned man had become so preoccupied with the delightful thought of revenge that he had forgotten all sense of time.

More than likely, LeFarge thought, Rolf was making Raider suffer endlessly before he received the final mercy of death.

LeFarge smiled into the night. He had, after all, taught Rolf well about such things. The teaching had been a pleasure, and he regretted now that he had not saved Raider for afterward so that he himself could have participated in the long and painful conclusion to the man's life. Pain delivered to a man was, after all, nearly as good as that given to a woman. Just thinking about it gave Charles an erection.

There was no ease for that problem at the moment. But tomorrow he would take care of it. He smiled, more broadly this time.

Lady Judith seemed not quite so dependable as he had expected. Her actions and her attitudes lately hinted that she had developed a genuine fondness for this Raider person.

And Charles had promised her that she could join her recent lover when this business of the gold was concluded.

It was a promise Charles fully intended to keep. Rolf was even now sending Raider on his journey. Tomorrow Charles would send Judith to join him.

Then, oh yes, his potency would be enormous.

His imagination and his actions could meld totally, and he could allow himself limitless use of her senses.

Charles laughed, thinking about the airs she sometimes assumed. And all this time she had thought of him as a gentleman born, just as she had been born to the peerage.

If only she knew, he thought with anticipation. Well, tomorrow she would know. He would tell her himself. All of it. And oh, how sweetly she would suffer until that knowledge—like all else—left her. In slow, slow death.

He shuddered, thinking about it, and his erection was painfully insistent.

In the meantime, though, that damned Rolf was having entirely too good a time with the disposal of Raider. It was taking him simply too, too long. He should have been here by now to oversee the placement of the powder charges.

By now Charles should have been able to turn over field command of the operation to Rolf so that he himself could retire to Leadville and a public display of his own obviously innocent presence at the time the robbery occurred.

Never before had Charles physically participated in the execution of one of his plans. Alway's that had been Rolf's responsibility.

But now Rolf was late, and Charles was becoming annoyed. Not worried, certainly. Charles was fully capable of handling the smallest detail of any of his plans. Otherwise how could he hope to properly supervise his personnel.

But he was, he admitted to himself, annoyed.

Charles looked at his watch. It was so dark now that he had to strike a match to be able to read the face of the excellent timepiece.

Five minutes until ten. Already the individual mines would be transporting their portions of the shipment to the depot for the ten P.M. loading schedule. And still no Rolf.

Charles walked out onto the track, the steel rails gleaming silver in the moonlight, and listened for the approach of Rolf's footsteps. He could hear nothing except the low talk of his men in their hiding places nearby.

He could wait no longer. Charles would have to oversee the placement of the charges himself. Worse, he would have to remain here during the attack on the train. There was no longer time for him to return to Leadville and show himself at a gaming table for witnesses to see and remember.

Charles had mixed feelings about that necessity. He had always wisely demanded the protection of witnesses to his innocence. But in truth he had always missed the excitement of the actual kill.

So now, minutes before the most devastating of his careful plans, he was both distressed by this last-moment change and excitedly pleased that this one time he would be an actual participant in the carnage and the theft.

That prospect too affected him, and his erection returned harder and more pulsatingly demanding than ever before.

"Bickley," he said softly into the darkness.

"Yes, boss?" The answer came from startlingly close beside him.

"Bring the powder and come with me. Ross, you may begin laying out the wire."

"Right," another voice whispered. Really there was no need here for silence, but both anticipation and training demanded it nonetheless.

Two shadowy figures showed themselves, one bent over with a reel of light wire, the other carrying a heavy pack slung over his shoulder. Ross began to lay wire from the already positioned battery box toward the wooden supports of the tall, spindly bridge; the other joined Charles on the tracks.

Charles led the way out into the center of the short span and climbed quickly over the side. By now, he was thinking, soon-to-die guards in Leadville would be loading crates of unrefined but already nearly pure gold onto the cars. He smiled into the darkness as Bickley began to hand down bag after bag of powder.

Charles accepted the bags one by one and, working by feel, wired them in place at the weak knee junctions of the trestle.

He fitted explosive caps with preattached wire leaders into position on each of the charges, then reached up for the blocks of light sculptor's clay that he pressed around each charge to shape and contain the explosions.

By the time Charles was done placing and shaping the charges needed to buckle the trestle, Ross was there with the wire.

One by one, being very careful of his connections, Charles attached the battery box wire to the blasting cap leaders.

The danger of it excited him. It also worried him. If even one of the charges should go while he was still there working on them . . .

He stopped himself from asking the question about whether Ross had remembered to leave the other end of the wire unattached from the battery box so there could be no possibility of an accidental discharge. `

The question would have been an admission of weakness. And Charles permitted himself no displays of weakness. Never. Not to Rolf. Not to his men. Not to anyone.

He completed his task and climbed back onto the railway. He felt exhilarated and confident.

Perhaps, he thought, he had made a mistake all this time in removing himself from the scenes of his escapades. The danger was greater this way, it was true. But the satisfactions were immeasurably larger as well.

From now on, he thought, he just might have to join his men in their work.

He smiled and led the way back into the positions of hiding that had chosen days earlier.

Charles himself knelt to connect the wire to the terminals of the huge, heavy battery box.

He looked at his watch again and was assured that by now Andrew would already be on his way to the rendezvous point with the two trains of mules, one train with empty packs ready to receive the gold, the other train already loaded with ballast rock so they could lay a convincing false trail for the foolish authorities to follow.

Everything, *every*thing, Charles thought, was going perfectly this night.

Far up the track Charles could see the yellow gleam of a headlamp come into view.

Another half minute and he could hear the powerful clatter of the steam engine that was working so dilgently to pull wealth into Charles's grasp.

Charles smiled and reached down to touch himself. This excitement, he thought, was very great.

"Ready now," he called softly into the darkness. "They come."

# CHAPTER TWENTY-FOUR

The roar of the water filled Raider's ears, and the aching pressure in his chest threatened to flood his mind with panic as well.

Even during those few, fleeting seconds when the whimsy of the water tumbled them into the air, Raider could not breathe. Rolf's iron grip on him was too strong. It was crushing him.

Raider held his breath—he had no choice—and tried to knee Rolf in the balls.

They spun through the torrent, underwater again, and Rolf's hold became even tighter from his fear.

They had entered the very worst of the rapids now. Locked together, the two men were thrown and tossed like a bauble in a giant's uncaring hand.

Foam streamed over them as they broached into the air once again, and Raider shoved searching fingers deep into Rolf's nostrils before the man could take a breath.

Rolf's mouth gaped open as he sought oxygen, and the two of them were shoved underwater by the awesome force of the river.

Raider could feel Rolf's massive chest heave in protest as the water entered his lungs.

For a moment, for one scant, delicious moment, Rolf's grip eased, and Raider gulped in a mouthful of sweet, exhilarating air as the vagaries of the river threw them upward.

They were being swept downstream at a terrifying pace. As they struggled, Raider's fingers still socketed deep inside Rolf's nose and his thumb searching for Rolf's eye, Rolf squeezed, trying to crush Raider's rib cage, and the river tumbled and turned them.

The water brushed them past a protruding rock. Raider's shoulder grazed the rock, numbing his entire arm and making him lose his grip in Rolf's face.

The impact spun them, twisting them, so that Rolf's back faced downstream, Raider's toward Leadville far upriver.

Their bodies breasted a white-water wave, and Raider could see for a moment past Rolf's shoulder. He ducked his head and buried his face against Rolf's throat.

The torrent flung them viciously forward. Onto the proud, jagged boulder Raider had just glimpsed.

Rolf was driven heavily onto the upstream side of the rock.

Its forward edge slammed him in the spine.

Raider could feel the impact of their two bodies dashing against the unyielding stone.

Even over the roar of the rapids he could hear the muffled crack as Rolf's spine broke.

The big man's arms dropped away, and Raider was spun free, whirling and plunging around the side of the boulder and down into the foaming water beyond it.

His head bobbed into the air, and he gulped in life-giving breath before the water closed over him again.

His right arm was numb and useless, but even if it had not been, no man could ever have hoped to swim against the terrible power of that raging current.

Raider reached out with his left arm and began to stroke *with* the flow of the river, angling only slightly toward the bank and toward safety.

White water spewing into the air yards in front of him warned of another boulder, and he twisted to the side, presenting the rock with his already useless right arm and shoulder.

The river pulled him around it, and again he began to stroke toward the bank, riding with the river instead of uselessly trying to fight it.

Foaming water leaped and danced and dragged him under time after time, but each time he fought his way back to the surface and patiently stroked downstream at a narrow angle.

A rock caught him on the hip and spun him sideways. The water pushed him under, and his knee banged nastily against sharp gravel.

The impact hurt. It also gave him hope. He was close enough to the bank now to touch bottom if he could only get his feet under him.

He stroked forward again, and a wall of falling water closed over him and pushed him under.

Raider came up sputtering and gasping, thrashing the water with his left arm and trying once again to stroke for safety.

It took him several seconds to realize that the water he was flailing with his good arm was calm and smooth.

He lay in an eddy, the rage of the rapids several feet away in the channel of the Arkansas.

Raider relaxed and allowed himself to float. Tentatively he felt downward with his booted feet. He found gravel there.

Weary and sore but still alive, he came first to his knees and then to his feet. He waded out into the bank, shivering from cold and aching in every joint and muscle.

But he was alive.

He stood there in the last fading light of the day and searched the white, leaping surface of the river for some sign of Rolf. He did not find it. The river had claimed him as its booty and had taken Rolf to its icy depths.

Raider shook himself and shivered. Then he turned and began to walk upriver as quickly as he could force himself.

He limped and he swore, but he was in motion.

He had no time to waste on inconsequential matters like recovery from his ordeal.

Doc was gone, down in Denver now that he was needed. If Operation Snare was to be salvaged now, it was going to be Raider who would have to do it.

"Lordy," Raider breathed. He shivered not from cold but from a deep-rooted reluctance to do what he knew must still be done.

He stood on the bank of the river and glared at its smooth, oily surface.

Downstream a hundred fifty yards, no more than that, moonlight reflected on the white boil of another rapids. Upstream there was still another.

In front of him lay a relatively calm patch of water, but the calm was deceptive. Raider knew too well the power and speed of that current.

It could bear him down into the next rapids with terrifyingly casual ease.

But he had to get across. There was no better place. The suspension footbridges were impossibly far away, and he had no time now to reach them.

The headlamp of the train was already in sight as the gold shipment pulled slowly out of Leadville.

The train was driving now toward death.

Two dozen men or more would die tonight if that train rolled out onto the trestle LeFarge had mined.

And Raider knew it.

With one last, agonizing glance toward the approaching train, Raider threw himself into the river and began swimming with all the waning strength he had.

His right arm barely functioned, and his ribs felt like someone had spent the last week pounding on them with a shingler's wicked hammer.

His lungs were still rasping from the abuses they had suffered, and his belly knotted and churned from the river water he had ingested.

But he had no choice. He had to get across the Arkansas and reach the tracks before the train passed him on its way south toward certain death and destruction.

The river took him into its grip, and Raider swam across the channel at an angle, fighting for every inch of forward purchase, being swept three feet downriver for every foot he gained across it.

Over the sound of the nearby rapids he could hear the mournful hoot of a whistle as the caboose cleared the out-shirts of Leadville and the train began to pick up speed.

Raider drove himself harder against the pull of the river.

He had no choice if any of those men were to live until dawn.

# CHAPTER TWENTY-FIVE

Charles LeFarge smiled and reached for the plunger of the battery box. He stood and braced himself. The upward pull against the drag of the magnetos contained within the box was surprisingly difficult. The T-handled plunger felt heavy. It resisted his pull.

He drew the arm up to the top of its travel and stood poised over it.

As soon as the engine reached a point fifty feet from the north edge of the trestle, he would blow the charges.

He had calculated that distance long since.

The charges would drop the span almost instantly, and there would be no way for the engineer to react in time to slow the speed of the train before the engine and each of the following cars plunged sixty feet into the dry bed of the creek where his men waited.

The only thing Charles had not been able to calculate for certain was the jackstraw manner in which the following cars would fall.

He hoped they would spread out, allowing each a nicely death-dealing distance to drop. But there was always the possibility that one car might land on another and injure but not kill its occupants after falling a somewhat lesser distance. That was why it was so important to have his men there.

They, with Charles among them this time, could swiftly go through the bodies and dispatch any guard or train crewman not yet dead from the impact of the crash.

Charles rather hoped there would be some who did survive the wreck.

He wanted for himself the pleasure of finishing them.

He was thinking about that, thinking that perhaps he could borrow a knife from one of his men—most of them carried a knife—and thus receive more immediately personal pleasure than would be possible with a firearm.

With his thoughts thus preoccupied, it took Charles several moments to realize that the gold-carrying train was no longer steaming ahead at full speed.

The engine had begun to slow.

Indeed, he realized now, it had not been traveling at the high rate of speed he had expected.

In fact, the engine was braking now.

Cars clanked and groaned as railroad brakemen twisted the steel spokes of their brake wheels.

Steel shrieked against steel as the drag of the brakes set against the impetus of momentum and hauled the train protesting to a stop.

The engine came to rest a few feet from the end of the trestle span.

Charles realized too late.

He came to his feet, but already his eager men were pouring out of their hiding places to charge the cars.

Bright flashes of muzzle flame leaped from the sides and the roofs of the cars.

Rifle fire and shotgun fire and, worst of all, the rolling, almost continuous thunder and fire as two, three, five Gatling guns opened up on the members of Charles's gang.

All around him men began to fall writhing onto the harsh gravel soil as the bullets found their marks.

A few, pitiful few of Charles's men were able to return the devastating gunfire from the train.

Charles knew every position and every man who was firing from that train. Raider had told him about each and every one of them.

But it was too late now to concern himself with that.

The guards were still alive. They were not supposed to be.

The train itself sat strong and secure as a fortress on the tracks. This was not supposed to be.

Charles's men fired at the train and were cut mercilessly down by the gunfire from sandbagged emplacements on the undamaged cars.

The night was aflame with muzzle flashes, horrendously loud with the sharp, ugly reports of the guns.

Charles looked with horror at the destruction of his men.

He abandoned the now useless battery box and turned to flee wildly into the night, his arms and legs pumping and his chest smarting from lack of breath and, more, from an unnamed terror that pursued him with every racing step he took.

# CHAPTER TWENTY-SIX

Raider watched as the brakeman, pressed into service on the authority of the conductor, climbed back down the slender pine pole where the telegraph wire had been strung.

"You hooked it up just the way I told you?" the conductor asked.

"Yessir, jus' the way you said."

The conductor nodded. He was the only member of the train crew who could operate a telegraph key, and he was much too fat to have made the climb himself.

The man fed the wire through an open window into the lighted and reasonably comfortable caboose, then climbed awkwardly in through the door off the back platform. Raider followed.

Through the open windows Raider could see the guards, lanterns in one hand and weapons in the other, comb the rocky countryside nearby for surviving bandits. So far they had found very few who had survived the fusillade of gunfire from the train.

The conductor hooked up his key and tapped out a call sign for the Buena Vista operator.

"I have him," he told Raider.

Raider nodded. He began to dictate slowly, the train conductor laboriously tapping out the signals as Raider spoke.

"Robbery attempt thwarted. Gang members waiting with pack mules north of Buena near tracks. Send posse to intercept and arrest. Expected escape route via Poncha Pass, repeat Poncha. Please acknowledge. Signed Raider."

There was a wait of several minutes, then the conductor's telegraph key began to clatter.

The conductor sat with his head cocked toward the clickety-clack noise. He wrote the letters down as they came in and also slowly spoke each word as it was formed.

"Weatherbee... here... Stop... Local... authorities... forming... posse... now... Stop... Information... source ... located ... comma ... net ... of ... telegraph ... operators ... Stop ... Pinkerton ... Agency ... advised ... Stop ... Denver ... operator ... apprehended ... comma ... talkative."

Raider grinned. That damned old Weatherbee had been on the job after all, in his own plodding fashion.

The conductor continued speaking. "Hodding... supervisor... enroute... Leadville... re... MacDonald... Stop... Shall... accompany... posse... comma... join ... you ... Leadville ... ayem ... Stop ... Signed ... Weatherbee."

Raider smiled. He felt stiff and sore and miserable. And pretty damn good.

A burly guard, chief of the security force for the mine owners, stepped into the caboose. "I think we have them all now. There's only three still breathin'. My boys are fetching the dead ones up to load 'em on the flatcar."

"I better take a look," Raider said. He followed the man, whose name he could not remember, out onto the loose rock of the rail ballast. Just climbing down from the caboose hurt.

He limped forward to the flatcar with its sandbagged Gatling gun nests, and one of the guards held a lantern so Raider could get a look at the gang members both dead and alive.

He looked them over carefully and then a second time just to make sure. He began to swear.

Charles LeFarge was not among them.

Raider hurried back to the caboose and found the conductor.

"We have to back up to Leadville," he said.

The conductor shook his head.

"Damn it, man," Raider protested. "Lefarge is still loose. If he gets away we won't have done a lick of good tonight. He'll just start all over with another gang."

"Sorry," the conductor said, "but that isn't my problem. My job is to get this shipment delivered safe to Julesburg. Then some other poor bastard takes over till it's signed in at San Francisco."

Raider argued with the man but to no avail. The train was going on on its scheduled route come hell or high water. After, that is, the bodies had been loaded and the powder charges removed from under the trestle. A crew of guards from the mines, knowledgeable about powder and fuses, were at work now clearing the charges.

Raider cussed some more and looked helplessly out into the night.

He was just too damned stiff and hurting to walk all the way back up the tracks to Leadville.

"Shit," he muttered.

He left the caboose and went back out to find the security chief. If nothing else, at least maybe someone would lend him a damn gun.

Raider dreamily returned to consciousness. He felt like he was in the river again. But this time it was not cold and frightening.

This time he floated softly on it, gently, surrounded by warmth and wetness.

The heat and the moisture, oddly, were centered at his groin.

It was almost like...

He blinked and came fully awake. And smiled.

Yeah, he was surrounded by warm and wet, all right.

But it was no damn river that was pulling at his cock.

That was Judith's gleaming hair that was draped over his balls. And while he couldn't exactly *see* what she was up to, thanks to all that hair hanging like a curtain over his belly, he could sure *feel* what she was doing.

My oh my, he thought. The lady was right good at it, too.

He reached down to stroke the back of her head, encouraging her.

She sucked him in deeper and tickled his balls with sharp, lightly applied fingernails, almost driving him out of his mind with the combined pleasures.

He could feel himself building, building...

The hotel room door slammed open, and a grinning son of a bastard of a Weatherbee marched boldly in.

The old fart was no longer burdened with the padding and grimy clothes of his disguise. He looked disgustingly healthy and rested.

Raider himself felt like shit and could have gotten no more than a few hours of healing sleep so far.

Damn him.

Raider's expression of pain seemed only to add to Doc's pleasure at being able to interrupt him.

Judith, flushing a bright red, squealed and retreated under the sheets, huddled into a ball at the foot of the bed with the covers pulled tight around her.

Her sudden departure left Raider's tool quivering unattended in a reach toward the ceiling.

Raider glared at Weatherbee and felt himself begin to droop. "Bastard," he mumbled.

"Something wrong?" Doc asked cheerfully. "Of course not. Why, think about it, Rade. The railroads might even

give us a bonus for this performance." He grinned and
pointed toward Raider's still wet but no longer ready mid-
section. "Not, I think, for that one. But probably for the
other."

"What the hell do you want?" Raider demanded.

Doc managed to look innocently wounded. "You know
good and well that we have to get our report off, Rade."

"So quit bothering me an' make the damn thing," Raider
said.

Doc perched happily on the side of the bed and turned
an inquiring eye toward the motionless lump in the covers
at the foot of the bed. He said nothing about that, however.

"First I have to assemble all the pertinent facts," he said.
"You might want to know, for instance, that the mule train
was successfully located. There were four packers. Three
of them are now in jail. The fourth was foolish enough to
resist. There was, I regret to say, no sign of LeFarge with
them."

Raider grunted.

"Have you anything to add?"

"Never occurred to you, I reckon, to go check with the
local sheriff."

"Is that gentleman obligated to report to Pinkertons?"
Doc asked innocently. "I think not. Therefore, Rade, I come
to you for my information."

Raider considered throwing something at the prick. But
he had nothing to throw.

There was, of course, the revolver hanging at the headboard. But even Raider considered that a trifle extreme.
Regretfully he dismissed the idea of shooting Weatherbee.

"If you had bothered to check," Raider said with a pa-
tience he did not feel, "you would find Mon-sewer LeFarge
behind bars and ready for trial an' likely hanging. If you'd
bothered to check, that is."

"Really? And how might that have happened? Did he
turn himself in, seeking sanctuary from you?" Doc was
grinning enough to tip Raider that the bastard had already
*known* LeFarge was in jail.

But if Raider accused him of it, the sorry SOB would

only deny it. Raider was not going to give him that satisfaction.

Remembering, though, Raider realized what a close call
it had been when he finally limped his way back to the hotel
around dawn.

Not for himself but for Judith, who was still huddled out
of Doc's sight at the foot of the bed.

He had found her with that prick LeFarge but no longer
as the bastard's mistress.

She had become his victim.

The son of a bitch had had her tied up like a hog ready
for slaughter and gagged so she couldn't cry out.

She was naked, and so was LeFarge, the man's thin little
pecker standing out like a tiny red candle on a Christmas
tree.

LeFarge had already started to whip her with the buckle
end of a belt, and he had an assortment of nasty-looking
implements laid out to turn to when he got tired of seeing
her writhe and squirm from the impact of the belt.

Judith had already been welted and bruised and was
bleeding.

Her back would likely be scarred for the rest of her days,
and one pale, delicate breast had been laid open so bad that
Raider had had to take her for stitching up by a doctor
before he could bring her back to the hotel.

But she hadn't had to worry about LeFarge anymore.

It was just stinking damn luck that let him survive the
slug Raider had put into the asshole's balls.

Still, Raider reflected now, Judith was going to get better.
A little time and she would heal.

He smiled.

All the fucking doctors in France wouldn't be able to put
Charles LaFarge back together again.

"Weatherbee," he said, "it occurs to me that if ol' Charlie
LeFarge can live through what I done to him, you prob'ly
can too."

Raider reached toward the headboard.

Doc's grin disappeared. With a yelp of protest he jumped for the door.

Yeah, Raider thought. He just knew that son of a bitch'd known all about it to begin with.

Doc slammed the door on his way out.

Go send your silly reports, Raider thought. Take your time an' do it by the book.

He reached down and flipped the sheets back.

In spite of the salve-covered welts that streaked her fine body, Judith still looked . . . lovely.

Raider smiled at her and was delighted with the smile he received in return.

"Was there something you wanted t' finish, ma'am?"

He lay back and closed his eyes with a sigh while Judith returned to the task that had so recently been interrupted.

Yeah, he thought.

Yeah!

# J.D. HARDIN

"THE MOST EXCITING
WESTERN WRITER SINCE
LOUIS L'AMOUR"
—JAKE LOGAN

# JAKE LOGAN